MW00917785

THE ADVENTURES OF HARLEY EARLE

THE
ADVENTURES
OF
HARLEY EARLE

**By
Jerry Sibley**

Illustrations by Kayla Kiser

E-BookTime, LLC
Montgomery, Alabama

The Adventures of Harley Earle

This is a work of fiction. Names, characters, places and incidents either are the product of the author's imagination or are used fictitiously, and any resemblance to any actual persons, living or dead, events, or locales is entirely coincidental.

Library of Congress Control Number: 2006927321

ISBN: 1-59824-230-X

First Edition
Published May 2006
E-BookTime, LLC
6598 Pumpkin Road
Montgomery, AL 36108
www.e-booktime.com

This book was written for my grandchildren, so I dedicate it to them.

Rye Sibley
Ivy Sibley
Cason Sibley
Jordan Sibley
Lynnsey Joy Sibley
Graham Sibley
Conner Sibley
Madison Sibley
Cheney Sibley
Wilson Sibley
Julianna Steen
Jake Steen

——And——

Those to Follow

Contents

Contents

Foreword

My oldest grandchild is almost sixteen years old. There are eleven more that are younger than her. I have been in the homes of my two sons and my daughter many times at bedtime. Invariably, as these little darlings went off to bed, they asked the same question. "Daddy are you coming up to tell us a bedtime story?" The answer would always be, "Yes, I'll be up in a few minutes."

I decided that all of our grandkids need to hear some stories that are more real and lifelike than 'Little Red Riding Hood' and 'The Three Pigs'. After much thought and reflecting, I thought that I might be of some help by providing some new material for the overworked and stressed dads out there.

The main character in this book is named, 'Harley Earle'. His real identity is a secret to all, even to me, but I think he is a little bit of a lot of people. Some of the stories in the book actually happened, but not necessarily and exactly as they are recorded. Therefore, I must impress on you, that everything written on the following pages is fiction and written to catch the imagination of the kids that hear it.

The names of some characters in the book are names of people that are special to me and I use their names only to honor them.

I must say again, this is totally a book of fiction and even the stories that seem to be factually true are most times embellished, just a bit.

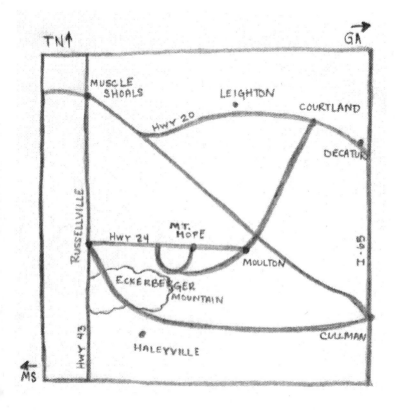

EARLY DAYS IN MT. HOPE

Where's hope?

Believe me there are always times in our lives that we wake up in the morning and wonder, where is hope and is there any hope out there? Good news. There is and it is here. Where is here? In fact, hope is where we are. God saw to that.

I don't want to get too deep in the scriptures just now. That will be for another day. Today I just want to relate to you a story that happened yesterday or was it yesteryear? Yesteryear I think. Do you remember a kid whose name was Harley Earle? He was the kind of person that gives us hope. Most of us old timers remember him or his escapades quite well. You see, Harley was the kind of boy that was sort of overlooked by the elite of our town. People just never gave much thought to one who was named 'Harley'. They also thought such names as Claude, Clyde or Clovis didn't add much to ones resume either.

Lets get back to Harley Earle. He was comfortable in his overalls and red flannel shirt. This kid woke up early every morning with a new goal in mind. He liked to do exciting things and was always looking for something new to do. Some times Harley did things that were almost wrong, but not enough wrong to get him in trouble. He had a kind heart and loved God.

A certain morning in the fall of 1950 he had the urge to hunt for arrowheads in the mountains. Harley put on his school clothes and ate his breakfast. With his backpack filled with a few extra crackers and peanut butter he was ready for the school bus. He got on the bus on the side away from the house every morning. This morning he was waiting on the loading side when the bus pulled to a stop. The door opened and Harley Earle told the driver to go on that his dad was going to bring him to school later. The bus pulled away and Harley jumped into the deep ditch behind him.

After a while he ran down the ditch until he was out of sight of his house. Then it was on to the big mountain. As he waded across the treacherous Tannyard Creek, his canteen was filled with good spring water. Then it was on to his hunting grounds.

Soon he reached the foot of Eckerberger Mountain. The mountain seemed to be much taller looking at it from the bottom than seeing it from his front porch two miles away.

Harley took a deep breath and started to find a path that would not be too exhausting. Soon he was halfway up the mountain and was starting to feel a little tired. He noticed that there was a really old birch tree off to one side of the path he had chosen. The tree looked interesting to him and worth looking at a little closer. Upon closer examination he saw names and dates carved into the bark of the huge tree. There was one that said "1863 Battle of Mt. Hope." There was another that said Pvt. T. J. Sibley. And then there was a heart with an arrow through it. The thought of a battle stimulated his imagination. He thought that a little rest would be in order just now and he lay down on a patch of soft grass. A few minutes later he was fast asleep and dreaming about the heroic days he fought in the 'Battle of Mt. Hope'.

The Yankees are coming, the Yankees are coming, was the cry of the people in the streets of Mt. Hope. They were a peaceful people and didn't understand why there was war in their country. The Union troops had crossed the river and had fought their way up through Courtland. They were on their way to Mt. Hope.

HARLEY EARLE'S FIRST DREAM

The evening sky was the color of a ripened pumpkin. This was probably caused by the dust from the horses and mules of many Union troops. We had heard for days that the Yankees were coming and they were probably about a week away. There were probably around 5000 of them and were quite capable of stirring up a lot of dust. They were on their way to Moulton, then to Mt. Hope and then on to Russellville. When they finished their raiding there, it was on to Tuscumbia. We knew their plans pretty well but there was not a lot we could do about their plan to come through Mt. Hope which was located on the Byler road. This was the interstate of that time. Our scouts had told us that the Yankees were traveling up toward Moulton from the plantation area around Courtland and Hillsboro. We knew there were many large cotton fields ready to be planted. The open grounds would be good traveling for them but this many men and mules would leave the sky filled with red dust. We were later told that many large herds of cattle were killed. Some were carved up for their food but more were killed just to keep the southern plantation owners from feeding their own troops.

This part of the Union Army was led by the very ruthless and cruel Abel Straight. As far as he was concerned, his mission was to leave nothing worth a dime for the rebels to use in any later battle. Beautiful homes were burned. Crops and cattle were killed as they made their way on to Moulton and then on to Mt. Hope. Moulton was a thriving community, largely because of the money generated by a huge moonshining operation. People from far off states came to Moulton to buy their liquor. This was the main source of income for most of the people there. Most people thought it was because of the good spring water that was so readily available in the area. The owner of the large still where the 'shine' was made was the most respected man in the community, except the sheriff, who by the way, was his brother. He was respected because he shared his profits with all the people in town that needed any help. He was especially good to the preachers. He was a good tither and always supplied plenty of juice for the communion days. Well, you can guess what happened when the troops made their way into Moulton. First, all the 'shine' that was at the still was drank up and a huge fight broke out among the ones that didn't get any and the half drunk ones that did. After the fight was over, the Yankees looted and burned the town, still and all. The town has never been the same since. Once the income stopped the sheriff and his brother moved out to Double Springs where they started up a new still and prospered until they died. The Yankees later camped there, but did not destroy the town.

Soon, Col. Straight and his men left Moulton. Then it was up the mountain and on to the Byler road. We again had word that the 'Yankees' were coming. The local leaders had a meeting and decided to take everyone's cattle and other livestock far into the mountains to hide them. We knew if they were left at our farms that they would kill them all. We also loaded up all the valuables we had and hid them in the mountains also.

Mt. Hope was a really prosperous town in 1863 before the Yankees came. There were several dry good stores, a dentist, two doctors, three barbers, three cafes, four schools, one undertaker, a post office and two cotton gins.

When the Union soldiers were finished with us, there was little left. We fought the best we could, but there were so many of them we just didn't have a chance. Most of our boys were away fighting in other battles. When I came to from being shot in the belly I was on top of Eckerberger Mountain. About that time a squirrel ran across Harley's leg and woke him up. He realized he had dozed off to sleep and dreamed about the Union troops coming to Mt. Hope. In any case, he was glad the Harley in his dream was not killed in the battle.

Harley realized that he was a little hungry and decided to eat the crackers and peanut butter he had prepared earlier and then go on up the mountain.

Where is the Soapstone Cave?

WHERE IS THE SOAPSTONE CAVE?

As Harley Earle began to go on up the mountain, he began to feel a little chill in the air and just a tinge of hunger. The peanut and butter and crackers he had eaten earlier had about played out. He decided it would be best for him to go back down the mountain and prepare to "get off the bus." Soon he was back to the deep ditch in front of his house. He decided that the bus really needed to stop in front of his house in order for his mom to think he was arriving home from school. How was he to get Uncle Gus to stop the bus just in time to make it all work out. He realized that there was a pumpkin patch across from the house and ditch that he was hiding in. He quickly crawled out in the patch and selected a couple of pumpkins that Uncle Gus could see from a 100 feet away. That would give the him plenty of time to stop. Harley carefully rolled the pumpkins out into the middle of the road. Soon he heard the old rickety bus coming. Harley quickly jumped into the deepest part of the ditch and watched as the bus slowly rolled to a stop. Ray and L. O. Jumped out and got the two pumpkins and Uncle Gus ground the gears into action and the bus went on it's way. As the bus was going around the curve, Harley was already on the front porch and hollering to his mom that he was ready for his afternoon snack.

After his snack, Harley always took a few minutes to rest from his busy day at school. As soon as he stretched out he began to think about what he was going to tell his dad when he came home and started to ask him about his day at school. He knew it would be wrong to tell a fib. Maybe he would not ask him anything. He sure hoped that would be the case. Harley always seemed to drop right off to sleep when he got still and he did this time also.

The dream that he was having on the mountain started right up again. Harley, the soldier, healed quickly. He was soon able to pick us his old musket and head on up the mountain. He knew that the Yankees had ransacked the Templeton plantation and were eating the best food from Mammy's food pantry. Mammy was the Templeton's cook.

He later heard that the union troops were so cruel that they killed all Dr.Templeton's hogs and cows, even though they only needed a few for their food. They didn't hurt any mules as they were taken with them to ride on to the next battle.

Harley had heard his dad and granddad talk about Soapstone Cave. It had always been his aim to someday go to that place because there were so many different yarns that had been spun about it. He knew it was somewhere near the middle of Eckerberger Mountain and that was about all he knew about it's location. He had heard about the very soft white stones that had been found there. One yarn was told about the stones being used for soap.

As he drug his old rusty musket on up the mountain he began to notice that some of the trees had a notch on them. He began to follow a trail that had the notched trees along its side. Soon he was further into the scary mountain than he had ever been before. It had been several days since he was injured in the Battle of Mt. Hope. He thought he was almost as strong as he was before the battle.

Around mid afternoon walking on the trail became a little painful. The Yankees had taken his boots and all that he had on his feet was shoes made from bark and some rawhide strings. Ever what was under the leaves on the trail was sharp and painful to his feet. He knelt down and brushed away the leaves. The path was covered with hundreds, perhaps thousands, of arrowheads. This was the Indians idea of a paved road, he guessed. Anyway, Harley knew that he was getting close to something, hopefully it was Soapstone Cave.

Then things changed. There seemed to be hundreds of thorn trees and briar bushes blocking the trail. Harley figured that this is where so many turned back. The Indians must have thought that the white man was a sissy and he would not venture on up the trail due to these obstacles.

Harley Earle would not be denied. He decided to go around the huge grove of thorns and briars. It must have taken the better part of an hour to go around the trail and get back on it. No sooner had he gotten back on the trail, he was scared out of his wits. He not only saw the entrance to a cave but in front of it he saw a huge bear guarding it.

Needless to say, Harley woke up hollering. His dad had come in about that time and he shook Harley's shoulder. About all Harley could say was, "I am hungry, what's for supper?" Harley could hardly wait to go to bed. He had to see what was inside Soapstone Cave.

HARLEY'S BUSY WEEKEND

Suppertime at Harley's home on Friday nights meant fried potatoes, pinkeye purple hull peas, boiled ham hocks and corn bread. It had been a long and tiring day and the boy was hungry as a bear. This night he was good for two helpings of everything. A full stomach left him so sleepy that he was sound asleep before the "Lone Ranger" story came on the radio. He was so full and tired he never dreamed one dream.

Saturdays were meant for fishing when the weather was good. After waking up, Harley knew what his first task was to be after breakfast. He knew to get an old salmon can and a shovel and head to the barn for worm digging. When he had dug a full can of wigglers he would look for a few crickets. And then as soon as dad was finished with milking the two jersey cows, they were ready to go. There was something different about this Saturday morning. Harley would have preferred to stay home and take a nap. Be couldn't wait to finish his dream about Soapstone Cave.

The fishing went pretty good and when the fish stringer was full, he was ready for the Saturday night fish fry.

Another thing that happened on Saturday was the 'Saturday night bath'. This particular night he hurried to get the water heated on the cook stove and the tub filled. This was going to be a quick one. As soon as he was dried off, he was off to bed. He tossed and turned but sleep just would not come.

He lay there and finished up his Saturday night listening with his dad to the 'Grand Ole Opra'. When the lights were out he finally dropped off to sleep. The next thing he was aware of was the smell of ham and eggs that mom was cooking in the kitchen. After a big breakfast, it was time to get ready for Sunday school and preaching. He thought that this Sunday, preaching would not be so bad. You see, Harley sometimes went to sleep during the preacher's sermons. It would please Harley to nap a little and maybe even catch up on his dreaming. This Sunday, things really went well for Harley. The preacher was really dull and he was asleep in no time at all. Sure enough, the dreaming picked right back up at Soapstone Cave.

About this time the preacher began to loosen up. He was beginning to really get into the sin nature of his people. Brother Ben shouted out a question to his flock, 'is there one out there that has sin in their life and wants to go to hell?

About that same time Harley was getting close to the bear. He stumbled over a dead limb and fell close to the hairy beast. One of the bear's arms fell across him and he started to holler at the top of his voice, no, no, no. He awoke from his dream as he heard the preacher say to him, "Harley, I am so glad to know you are brave enough to confess your sins openly and wish to be saved from the eternal fire. Come on up here son and pray with me." Well, Harley was so upset about wakening up from his dream and not being allowed to go on into Soapstone Cave that he almost swore off religion. He sort of waved the preacher off and slid down in the pew. He did decide that he had better listen to the rest of the preacher's sermon. He did not want to be caught off guard any more today.

As the family was going home, his dad asked him if he wished to talk to him about something. He thought Harley had been acting strange lately. Harley said, yes dad. 'Have you ever heard of any big black bears living around here'? His dad said, yes Harley, 'there is a story about one that was up on Eckerberger Mountain many years ago and some Indians trapped him and had a great feast for several days. Indians came from many mountains to the feast. The story goes that they skinned him and stretched his hide around some tree limbs so as to make him look real'.

Harley couldn't believe his ears. This had to be the bear in his dreams. It was so important to now get back to his dream and see if the bear he had dreamed about was the one that his dad had told him about.

SUNDAY EVENING WITH
HARLEY EARLE

It was really not that Harley hated weekends, it was that just this particular weekend he had some other things that seemed more important to him than fishing or going to church. He decided to make the best of the situation and so he began to make some plans on the way home from church. He was going to eat fast and make a fast exit from the kitchen.

About the time Harley finished eating lunch, his dad reminded his mom that Aunt Matter and Uncle Gus were coming for a visit. Harley about fell out of his chair when he heard this. You see, Uncle Gus is the bus driver and he is probably going to let the cat out of the bag that didn't ride the bus the other day. What could he do, Harley thinks to himself? One thing for sure, he had to think fast.

Sure enough Uncle Gus and Aunt Matter pulled up in the driveway. Harley thinks he has only one chance and that is to tell a "big one." He ran out to the driver's side of the old truck and stands in front of the door. Uncle Gus was not able to get out of the truck with Harley standing there. Harley then starts to tell his fib. He said, "Uncle Gus you need to know something before you go in and talk to dad. My daddy has been sort of sick for a few days now and the other day mom thought if she fixed him up a "toddy" that it would make him well. The only thing is that daddy drank too much of it and was not able to get out of bed that morning that I didn't ride the bus. Mom wanted me to stay at home and help with him and do his chores. You don't need to say anything to dad about my missing school that day because he is so embarrassed about the whole thing. Uncle Gus, you know my daddy is not a drinking man, him being a deacon and all, it would just kill him if this got out. Now, can I count on you to not say anything about that day?" Well, Uncle Gus thinks for a minute and tells Harley that he had completely forgot that he didn't ride the bus that day, but no he would not mention the day at all.

Harley Earle felt awful. There he had told a big story all for nothing. The worst thing about it was that he had told it on his daddy. How could he ever get forgiveness for it? He finally decided that the least he could do was to go to Jesus and ask him to please speak to God and see if he could forgive him. That would be the first step. Then he would cut extra firewood for the cook stove. Then he would fill the rain barrel with well water that was used for baths. There would be some other things that he would think of later, but right now he just had to get on up on that mountain.

Harley thought if he got a little closer to where he thought Soapstone Cave was that if he could just take a little nap and maybe his mind would let him pick up where he left off at the last dream. Mom was in the kitchen washing the dinner dishes and Harley slipped up to her and told her that he was going for a walk and would be back in a little while. She told him that he did not need to walk alone close to that mountain because some strange sounds had been coming from that direction for a few nights. This caused a little uneasiness but he was so determined to go that he quickly put the warning aside. He filled his pockets with molasses cookies and slipped around the house so that his dad would not see him and ask questions about where he was going and maybe what he had been talking to Uncle

Gus about. Harley was beginning to learn about the guilt one has when one tells a whopper.

THE NEW MOUNTAIN TRAIL

Before long Harley was way down in the pasture near the Tannyard Branch. He jumped into the dried up little creek bed and now he could go toward the mountain without being seen from the road that went in front of his house. As he got to the road there was a big culvert that went under it. He crawled up into it. He had forgotten what his mom had said about the sounds coming from that direction. He quickly thought about it when he heard a wild screeching sound from inside the culvert. Out the other end of it he could see bats flying out of it. Boy, was he glad they didn't come out on the end he was on. The floor of the passage was slippery but he made his way on to the end of it and to the side of the road that the mountain was on.

As he ran on up the ditch and between the rocks, he began to get tired. The foot of the mountain was about two miles from his front porch. He decided that he could afford just a few minutes to rest since there was a big limestone rock just ahead that had a flat surface on its top. After all, any rock that was that big deserved to be climbed. There were markings on the boulder. There was one that said Col. Abel Straight, April 27, 1863. This made Harley a little nervous to think he was laying on a rock that the mean old Yankee soldier had carved his name on.

This was not a dream. He knew that the Yankees had come through Mt. Hope and destroyed much of it in 1863. He had learned this in his history class that Miss Gevetta had taught last year.

He decided that since it had been that long there would be little that the mean old Col. could do to him now. Just a little rest and on he would go. But, you know Harley, just give him a few minutes laid out flat and he was sound asleep.

Just as he had thought, the closer he was to the mountain, the more likely he was to dream about Soapstone Cave. So once more the image of the big black bear came back to him. Something had dropped on his arm. It was part of the black bear. As he scrambled to get up he accidentally stumbled into the rest of the bear. He could not believe what had happened. The big black bear just fell apart. It had only been the hide and fur of a once living bear stretched over some limbs. They had all rotted and now had no strength to hold up the bearskin. Harley slowly and carefully made his way around what was left of the poor old bear. He made his way on up the trail.

Soon he came up on another trail that looked like it had only been made in the last few months. It appeared that this trail was coming from around the backside of the mountain. This was just too much of a mystery to Harley. He had to follow the newer trail. It only meant that someone else must be hunting for Soapstone Cave besides himself.

As he quietly moved along the trail, he would stop and listen to see if he could hear any noises. Seems like in the back of his mind he could remember someone saying something about noises coming from the big mountain. The trail was leading around the tall mountain. From where he was now he could only see a few feet ahead. The growth of the trees was very thick. In fact it was so thick that you could hardly see the sky. At least it was cool.

It seemed to Harley that he could smell just a hint of smoke in the air. Where could it be coming from? On just a few hundred feet he went. What was that? Voices? As he crept on he failed to see a carefully laid trap for any varmint that would come along the trail. The first thing he knew, he was falling.

Yes, Harley Earle was falling from the big limestone bolder that he was taking a nap on. And he was also hearing voices and smelling smoke. The voices were those of Mr. Boty and Mr. Jimmy. They were looking for some lost cows and had stopped out by the road to roll a smoke from their Prince Albert tobacco can.

Harley reasoned that this was what he had heard and smelled in his dream. But he was not so sure. He would get back on that new mountain trail as soon as he could, but now he best get on back to the house.

HARLEY AND THE CAT CAPER

Harley, being the inquisitive boy that he was, walked over to Mr. Boty and Mr. Jimmy and began to ask questions about what they were doing. They told him that they were looking for a wildcat that they had heard hollering last night. They were afraid the big cat may get some of their little calves. Harley asked them if they had ever heard of any bears on the Eckerberger Mountain. They assured him that there were still bears up there. This sort of scared Harley but not enough to discourage him about his next climb up the mountain. In fact, he could not wait until that time came.

The only thing that he couldn't figure out was when he would be able to climb up there again. He decided that he may just have to settle for climbing the big limestone boulder again and taking a nap on it. Maybe he could dream some more about Soapstone Cave.

He remembered that his Uncle Avis and Aunt Minnie and their two boys were coming to his house later on that evening. They were all going to church together that night. Bro. Ben was bringing in a big time preacher from Memphis for the night sermon.

Harley began to hurry on toward home. He always looked forward to his two cousins visits. When he got home they were already there. The two boys couldn't wait to tell Harley what they had in mind for the church service. It seemed that they had sneaked a box of cats in the back of their dads old truck. They told Harley what they had in mind and he heartily agreed with them that this prank would be more fun than a barrel of monkeys if they could pull it off.

The cousins knew the layout of the church, since they had visited it several times before. Well, the visiting preacher was beginning to really get wound up. About this time, Arnold whispered to his mama that he needed to go outside to the outhouse. He told her that he was scared to go by himself and wanted Harley to go with him.

She guessed it would be the neighborly thing for Harley to go with him and so the two slipped out of the pew and out the front door. Arnold and Harley then made their way to the old truck and got the box of very wild cats. They then went around to the back of the church and began to very quietly open the door. It was hid from the worshippers because of the choir curtains.

The evangelist was just getting to the convicting part of his sermon. He was preaching to the congregation that he was led to believe that there were demons in and around the church. The believers were really listening to what he had to say. No preacher had ever expressed their opinion that there might be demons in their little country church. He said that tonight that the people needed to pray the demons would leave the church so they could get on with the Lord's work.

When the top of the box was opened, the cats began to claw and scratch the boys. It was time for Harley and his cousin to release the box of nervous cats or get scratched really bad. They let them all go. Through the back door they went. They began to run around the choir area and around the feet of the visiting preacher. That did it for that sermon. The preacher ran for the front door and so did most of the worshipers. As the preacher ran for his car, they could hear him hollering. "Thank you Lord! Thank you

Lord, for letting me get out of that church without one of them demons biting me!"

Harley's daddy was not easily fooled. He began to look for his son and his cousin Arnold. After looking around the choir loft, he decided that someone had turned the cats loose from a box that was found just outside the back door. He examined the box and found a mailing address on it. The box had come from Sears and Roebuck. It had been mailed to Avis and Minnie.

Since Harley and his cousin had left the service to go to the outhouse together, there was no other explanation needed. Harley and his cousin had been the ones behind the cat-caper.

Brother Ben was most upset since every one had left the church before the deacons had a chance to take up the offering. Harley's daddy said to him, "Brother Ben, don't you worry about the offering, I am going to pay the visiting preacher from my own pocket."

Harley and the
Indian Village

HARLEY AND THE INDIAN VILLAGE

On the way home from church Harley was both scared and excited. He and Arnold had just pulled off one of the best pranks that had ever been pulled off in Mt. Hope. This one would be talked about for years to come. The only thing was that his daddy had not mentioned anything about what had happened. The other thing was that he was trying to figure out how he was going to explain all the scratches he had on his hands and arms.

When they all arrived home, Uncle Avis and Aunt Minnie gathered up their things and told the boys to get back in the truck. Harley believed that they must have figured out what had happened and just thought it best to take care of the matter when they got home. Arnold kept his hand behind his back so the bloody scratches would not cause questions.

Sure enough, Harley's fears were well founded. His daddy asked him to join him on the back porch. Of course, Harley had no choice but to join him except to possibly run away to Arkansas or maybe even to Florida. It would be warmer there. He guessed the best thing to do was to go on to the porch and face the music.

His daddy started the conversation by asking him a question. Harley, how did you like tonight's sermon? Harley stumbled and stuttered that he thought it was one of the most lively sermons that had been preached in that church in a long time. His daddy asked another question. Do you think God was pleased with the service?

Harley was beginning to feel really guilty by this time. He told his dad that he thought God might punish ever who let all them demons loose in the church. His daddy said he thought so too.

Harley was told by his father that he would go to school and come in each evening and stay in his room except to do his chores. He was not to go out to play or squirrel hunt or fish on Saturday or to play marbles or ride old Dolly or to do anything that was fun for the next week. At least, Harley thought, he did not tell him not to dream any dreams. Then he thought, boy I will have every evening after school to dream about Soapstone Cave.

Monday came and the bus was right on time. The kids on the bus sort of snickered when he took his seat. From the looks on their faces, they knew, they knew. The whole day was like that. All the girls snickered and laughed when Harley would walk by. The boys didn't snicker. They wanted to know all about what had happened and how did he pull it off.

The teachers, well that was a different story. They even suggested that maybe Harley could stay in at recess and catch up on some work that he missed last week. No marbles with Sam and Max that day. Finally, the bell rang and it was time to get on the bus for home.

Harley Earle was pretty sad until he remembered again that he would have at least six afternoons to dream. He was just dying to get back to that mountain but if he couldn't go in person, he could at least dream about it. The bus was in front of his house soon and as it screeched to a stop, he turned to his buddies and gave them a thumbs up and go off. He was on the porch and inside to kiss his mom and get a glass of milk and a cookie. He told his mom that he was glad that his daddy was punishing him because he deserved it. He told her that he was going to talk to the Lord that evening and ask him if he would once again forgive him

38

and that he would help him to be a better boy. Harley went on to his room and ate his cookie and drank his milk. Usually milk and cookies made him sleepy. It did this time also and as soon as he prayed to Jesus he began to drift off to sleep and in a few minutes he started to dream.

He dreamed he was climbing along the new mountain trail. As he eased along the path, sure enough, he got a whiff of smoke in the air. Where was it coming from? Another hundred feet down the path he began to see an opening in the trees. Up to this time he had not been able to see the sky because of so many big leaf trees.

There was an opening just ahead. As he got to the opening, he was so shocked to see what he saw that he almost fainted. There was an opening, perhaps as big as what we now know as a football field. It was filled with thirty or forty Indian teepees. There were Indians, old and young, walking around in the open space. Over to one side there was a patch of corn and what looked like a few rows of squash. There were several frames with animal hides stretched on them. The opening was in between three mountain peaks and it was impossible to see in or to see out.

There was one young Indian man that was grinding grains of corn on a big rock. Most likely it was his job to grind enough meal for the whole village. In another area, there were some women cutting and sewing the animal skins to make clothes for all the people. One old fellow was hoeing in the corn and squash patch. Way down at the end of the clearing, four young Indians were cleaning a deer that had been killed for their food. There was a spring of clear water there. Harley could almost taste the water from where he hid.

There was a sound behind him. He looked back and started to run but it was too late. Three young Indians had him surrounded before he knew what was happening. He knew the jig was up. Up went his hands and all the Indian talk he knew was the word ugh. When he said that word several times, the Indians laughed at him. After they stopped laughing, they said where did you come from, paleface?

They knew his language. This made him feel a little better. As soon as he could catch his breath he told them that he was looking for Soapstone Cave. A look of horror came over their eyes. What were they afraid of?

WAKE UP HARLEY

"Wake up Harley. Wake up Harley." He finally decided it was his mom hollering at him and not the Indians. He did not want to wake up. The dream was just getting interesting. It was time for Harley to go to the barn and start his chores.

He didn't mind milking Josey, but old Mable was trouble. She kept slinging her bushy tail, that was filled with cockleburs, around and hitting him in the face with it. Sometimes, Milkshake, the cat, would follow him to the barn. While he was milking, he would squirt the cat with milk. The cat didn't seem to mind. She would just sit down and lick it off her fur.

It usually took about ten minutes for Harley to milk each cow. He would get enough milk for the family to drink and some left over to make butter with. After the barn chores, it was back to the house and homework time. Today's homework was going to be interesting to Harley.

The story that he was to read and write a report on was about 'The Trail Of Tears'. This was about the rounding up of all the Indians out west and marching them through the states until they reached the swampy part of Florida. The Creeks and Cherokees had already been resettled several times but the white man kept on finding uses for the land that the Indians were living on.

There must have been over a hundred thousand Indians living in Oklahoma but some man from the east came through the country peddling trinkets and beads to the Indians and came upon several ponds of black sludge. He

41

recognized this as oil. He hurried back to New York and told his buddies about his find on the Indian reservations. They immediately began to figure out ways to get the Indians off that land.

A group of selfish men got laws passed to move the Indians to Florida. They promised them great riches there for their land in Oklahoma. They were promised sun, game, and riches if they would go. That was the start of the march called 'The Trail Of Tears'. It was named correctly because much sickness, hunger, and death took place on the trip.

As Harley began to read, his mind began to wander back to the Indians on Eckerberger Mountain. The story told of the trail that the Indians had traveled to the south. The trail came right through Waterloo, Alabama, and then on to Russellville, then right along the Byler Road. This was the road that was just on the other side of the mountain.

As the Indians were being marched along the road just above Mt. Hope a huge storm arose out of the southwest. The storm was called a tornado and it caused much confusion. The troops took cover anywhere that they could and temporarily forgot about the Indians. Well, the Indians had been in tornados before while living in Oklahoma and judged which direction it was traveling. They went sideways to the storm which led them to a low area in between what seemed to be three mountain peaks.

When the storm went on by, the soldiers began to round up the old and weak Indians. They were the only ones left as far as they could tell. The Yankee soldiers figured that the tornado had somehow blown away all the younger braves, squaws and their children.

The soldiers probably didn't care how many Indians that they delivered to Florida because they got paid for how many they started out with. Harley continued reading his homework assignment. It was a little more interesting than some he had been assigned to do. In the reading assignment he learned that a lot of the Indians escaped and hid in caves. One of the caves was called Soapstone Cave. When Harley read this, he sat straight up in bed.

Harley knew right away that the survivors of that storm were some of the ancestors of the Indians in his dream. He just had to get back to the dream and learn the rest of the story about the lost village. From the reaction of the three braves, they knew things about the cave that he had to also know.

HARLEY FINDS THE CAVE

Sleep would not come. Harley tried every thing he had ever heard about how to go to sleep. Naturally he tried counting sheep first. That didn't work. He counted to a hundred. Then he counted from a hundred back to one. That didn't work either. The night wore on and on. Finally after tossing and turning, he dropped off to sleep.

The next morning he was so angry. He had dreamed most of the night but the dream was about raising goats and sheep and about the time he and his cousin Arnold had shown their sheep in the local county fair. In the dream his sheep had a funny looking coat of wool. The sheep shearing clippers had not worked well and the little sheep's body looked really lumpy because of it. The people loved the way Harley led the lamb around the show ring but it was not enough to win a ribbon. The judges assured him that he would do better next year.

The next morning he was up and ready for school. He figured he would get on the bus and sleep on the way to school. Uncle Gus was a very slow driver, plus the roads were not suitable for much speed. The drive to school would take about an hour to get there. As the bus eased on down the road, Harley was looking out the window and it seemed like there was something bright up in the mountains, maybe like little flashes of light. Then he thought he could see a little smoke far off in the distance. If there was some way he could get off that bus he would find out what was out there.

He finally put it out of his mind and began to playfully pull Molly Sue's pigtail. Somehow he always managed to sit just behind her in order to pester the girl. She didn't seem to mind too much. After all Harley could run faster than anyone and could knock a softball further than anybody in their class. She thought he was a little bit cute.

The day at school drug on and on but eventually he was back home and having his cookie and milk. He was unusually sleepy this evening because of his restless time last night. Harley was drowsy and was soon asleep. The three braves, in his dream, took Harley, the paleface, down into the village. Now keep in mind the big storm had given the Indians a good chance to escape from the long walk to Florida. The braves didn't know for sure if Harley was looking for them or just what he had in mind.

Anyway they carried him to Chief Gold Tooth. He later learned that a dentist had filled the chief's tooth with gold when he was a young boy while he was on the Indian reservation.

The chief asked Harley if he was one of the soldiers that was leading his people on the trail to Florida. Harley assured him that he was not and that he was just out looking for a place in the mountains that was called Soapstone Cave. When he mentioned the cave to the chief he saw the same look of terror on his face that he had seen on the three braves' faces. What could be the reason for all the fear of the cave?

The Indians in the village gathered around Harley. They thought he talked funny. Some of the young squaws giggled at him. They led him around the village and showed him their tents that had been made from animal hides. They were really proud of their garden, especially their corn patch. They would take the grains of corn and beat on them on the top of a big rock that had a hole in it to catch the fine ground meal. This was used to make their bread with. The spring water that came out of the side of the mountain was cold and clear. The men had built a small house over the stream. As the water ran through it the house was cooled. This was where they stored the fresh meat and vegetables.

After a few days, Harley felt like he could ask the chief some questions about Soapstone Cave. At first the chief didn't want to talk about the cave. He finally asked Harley if he had ever heard of the 'Jessie James Gang'. Harley replied that he had heard of that the gang was bad news and liked to rob banks and other places. He told the chief that he never thought the gang would get to this area. The chief thought different. He believed that the gang was holed up in Soapstone Cave. This was a real shock to Harley. His enthusiasm for going there was dampened just a little.

He asked the chief if he and some of the braves would take him there. The chief said he would take it to the council and decide whether to go with him or not. The next day Harley, three braves and the chief started back up the path to the old trail that was to lead them to the cave. When they were about a mile from the cave, they began to see a little stream of smoke rising up through the trees. They began to walk very slowly and quietly. Harley thought he heard a mule braying. When they got close enough to the cave they could see that there was no one there, at least that they could see. On they went. The cave was big enough so that as many as ten horses could get in it. All the outlaws were gone. They had been there perhaps two or three hours earlier, but they were not there now. Chief Gold Tooth led them on into the cave.

Harley could hardly believe he was finally inside Soapstone Cave. It was huge. They went back into the cave until they could no longer see because of the darkness. As they made their way into the cave they began to find all kind of things that the James Gang had stolen. There was a trunk filled with all kinds of gold and jewelry. There was knives and forks made from the finest silver. They would probably melt these down later and sell as bars of silver. There were all kinds of guns and swords that the gang had brought to the cave.

Most likely, the gang had gone to rob another bank. They would not find much in the little town of Mt. Hope, so they probably had gone to Haleyville or Russellville. It was only about a day's ride on horseback to those towns. From the looks of the camp there must have been about five in the gang. There was a trail leading around the side of one of the mountains and it was not visible to anyone in the valley below. The gang could hide out in the cave for a long time before anyone would ever suspect anything.

Chief Gold Tooth was getting a little nervous and suggested that they had better leave before the gang came back. Harley did not want to go because he had not explored the cave enough. After much talking he decided it would be best to leave and comeback early some morning and explore while the gang was gone on another robbery. He would look forward to that day.

Harley heard those familiar words, "Wake up Harley! Wake up Harley! It's time to go milk the cows."

HARLEY STRIKES GOLD

Seems like the cows would take a day off ever so often, but no, they insist on being milked every day. Harley had learned in his F.F.A. class that cows usually were milked about ten or eleven months each year and then they would have a little calf. As soon as the little calf was able to eat grass and hay, it would stop suckling the mama cow and then someone like him would have to start the daily milking all over again. Most of the time his daddy would milk in the morning and he would milk the cows in the evening.

After the chores were finished, Harley knew it was time for him to start with the studies. It was about a week until report card time and he needed some good grades before then. Lately he had been thinking about other things rather than arithmetic and science. He did seem to like to read and study American History. It would even suit him to study all the next day but it would be Saturday and he knew his daddy had plans to dig the sweet potatoes up. They would have to be placed in the root cellar so they would keep through the winter. His family consumed a lot of the potatoes through the cold months and what was left were used as starters for next year. In the cellar they would sprout new baby plants which were pulled off and planted in May.

As old Tom and Ella, his daddy's mules, pulled the middle buster plow through the soil, Harley would pick up the potatoes out of the loose soil and pile them up. Later they would pull a sled down the row and put all the potatoes on it.

The digging was going good when suddenly Harley Earle hollowed out. "Stop the mules, stop the mules!" His daddy told old Tom and Ella to hold up. The mules stopped. They minded him better than Harley.

"Harley, what in the world is the matter? Why did you want me to stop plowing up the potatoes?" his dad asked.

Harley could hardly talk. Look dad, look dad what the mules uncovered. There must be a thousand dollars in this old can. His dad came back to where Harley was. He was busy digging in the loose soil. Another can. This time it was filled with coins. Where did all this money come from, he asked his dad?

By this time his dad also became excited. He got a shovel and started to help Harley dig a little deeper. The rains must have washed the soil away over the years because they had always had a garden in this spot. Six more cans were found with gold coins in them. By the time all the digging was completed, the mules were not needed. All the sweet potatoes had been uncovered.

The picking up would have to wait for another day. Gold coins had to be washed clean and counted. Harley's dad said not to worry with the paper money because it was old confederate dollars and had no value now.

Finding all this money just confirmed what he had earlier dreamed. He had also heard that the people that lived in the Mt. Hope Valley buried their valuables. Some hid them in the mountains when they heard that the Yankees were coming.

When the value of the gold coins were counted, the amount totaled $6,000. When the gold was turned in to the bank it was worth almost $22,000. Harley was instructed by his daddy that the discovery of the money could not be told to anyone. This was going to be a hard secret to keep.

Finding the gold seemed to cool Harley's desire to go back to Eckerberger Mountain. There was a new tractor to learn to drive and mama got a new home comfort cook stove. He was happy to just get a new bicycle. It had mirrors on the handlebars and mud flaps on the wheels. It even had a battery-operated headlight. The rest of the money, except the tithe, was put in the bank for Harley to use when he went to college.

Harley's daddy knew that if the news got out about the gold that people would be trying to dig up his whole farm to find more. He planned to do that himself in hopes of finding more. There was quite a stir in the church the Sunday that Harley's dad put in his tithe. He put it the plate up front when no one was looking.

When the preacher announced how many were in attendance that Sunday and then told that the offering was $2325.00, a big gasp sounded throughout the building. The offering was usually about $125.00. Someone must have put in $2200.00. Who in the world had that much money they all wondered. The new rich family never let on like they knew any more than anyone else. After the preacher preached a long sermon about giving to the church and how the giver would be blessed ten times over, they all went home.

Harley's family dined on sweet potatoes. This would always be their favorite dish.

Harley Picks Cotton and Dreams

HARLEY PICKS COTTON AND DREAMS

The following week was one that Harley always looked forward to. It was the week of Thanksgiving. That meant that he got out of school at the end of the day on Tuesday and did not have to go back until the following Monday. His dad always had the cotton picked by that time but there were always some bolls that opened later. Also in the low parts of the field the cotton stalks were real tall and there was a lot of newly opened bolls there. His dad would give him all the scrap cotton that he could pick while he was out for Thanksgiving.

As soon as he got off Uncle Gus's bus he ran to the house. He quickly ate his cookie and drank his milk, changed to his work clothes, and was away to the shed to get his picksack. He hoped to fill the nine-foot long sack with cotton before it got dark. He had big plans for the money that he would get for his cotton. He had heard that he could order from the mail order catalogue a new gadget that the F.F.A. teacher had told him about. The gadget was a metal detector. He just knew that if he had a metal detector he could find more buried treasure.

It was still hot for a late November evening. Nevertheless, Harley didn't slow down until he filled the long sack with cotton. The old cotton shed was still at the end of the field. This was where the cotton was weighed and emptied. He had picked forty-two pounds that evening.

He knew if he had a good day picking cotton tomorrow, he could get up to a hundred pounds more.

Then he would take off the next day to celebrate Thanksgiving with his cousins. There would probably be as many as twenty of them. The daddies would set on the porch or around a cedar and pine knot fire out close to the car shed. They talked about the war that had ended not long ago and about the big deer they had killed or about the big fish they had caught that summer. The mamas would finish Thanksgiving dinner and then wash the dishes. They were then ready to go into a room on the side of the house that was reserved for making quilts. They would start the quilting and talk over what they had been doing for the past year and other kinds of woman talk. Harley didn't know what the four girl cousins did, but they would get off to themselves and just giggle a lot.

The boys, well that was a different story. There was much mischief to get into. The first thing that they did was to go to the Tannyard Creek down behind the house. There is a long story about that creek that will be told later. The boys always liked to dam up the creek and back the water up all the way to the road. They used old tree limbs, mud and leaves to put in the way of the little creek's water. It just seemed to be fun for them to do this. After some other things were done during the evening, they would go back down to see how high the water had risen.

Harley had been saving all the corncobs for weeks for this day. Old Tom and Ella would eat all the corn off the cobs. They received twelve ears each day to eat. That meant there would be twenty-four new cobs every day. The big basket was running over with the cobs. Each cousin would be allowed to get his pockets full of cobs for the upcoming battle. They would choose up and one side was called the Rebels and the other side was the Indians. No one wanted to be a Yankee. The Rebels would go to the

North side of the barn and the Indians would go to the South side of the barn. The battle was soon underway. After about an hour and several black eyes, they got tired of throwing the cobs and were ready for some real fun.

It did not pay to be a cat on Thanksgiving Day at Harley Earle's house. There were always about ten cats around the barn. It was no accident that there was a basket of empty pork and beans cans back of the barn. The bales of hay provided plenty of string. Harley got a whipping almost every year after the company had gone home, usually for the mistreatment of the cats. To Harley it was worth the risk to see all those cats with cans tied to their tail.

This time they all ran under the house and the noise would cause quite a stir from the mamas inside. The men usually got as big a laugh out of the stunt as the boys did. Soon the day was over and all the kinfolks would go home. Harley always tried to stay out of sight after one of these days. He knew he was guilty of something wrong that he had done that day and would be called on to explain his actions.

He quietly went about his chores and slipped off to his room. He wanted to sleep long and good because he had plans to pick a lot of cotton the next day.

The day started just like Harley had planned it. He put some of the left over turkey and ham between some bread and fixed some peanut butter and crackers for his lunch and away he went to the cotton house. There was no dew that morning because it had been so dry lately. The sun was already up and the sky was blue. What else could a boy want if he had plans to pick a lot of cotton that day?

His sack was about half full of cotton when he got down in the real tall stalks. He shook the cotton to one end of his nine-foot long sack. He thought he just might rest a little. He did not want to give out too quick so he just lay back on the long sack. The cotton at the end of it was a perfect pillow.

Sleep came quick. Before long Harley was dreaming once again. He dreamed that he and the Indians were on their way back to their village after a brief visit to Soapstone Cave. He didn't view himself as a prisoner of the Indians so he felt that he would go along with them for a while and learn more about the village and the Eckerberger Mountain.

That night as they all sat around the campfire, Chief Gold Tooth told Harley about the horrible walk that they had made from Oklahoma. He said when he got to this part of the country he knew that this was where he wanted to be the rest of his life. When the storm came up he saw this as the chance for he and his people to escape. The soldiers that were guarding his tribe were all from up north and had never been in a tornado before so they all ran away from it in different directions. The chief said it was easy for them to get away in all of the confusion.

After much talk, the chief told Harley that they wanted him to be their blood brother. Harley said he thought that this would be a good idea also. The only thing was that he didn't realize that this would involve the shedding of blood. The chief sharpened his knife and told the braves to line up and hold out their hands. They did what the chief told them and he made a cut on each of their hands. He then came to Harley and told him the same thing. In order to be a blood brother their blood had to be mixed.

Harley couldn't take pain very well and about the time the chief cut his hand he hollered out. This caused Harley to wake up from his nap. He was enjoying the dream but he was glad to wake up because he had much cotton to pick.

HARLEY AND THE JESSIE JAMES GANG

This had been a good year for Harley. His grades had been fairly good. His family had been healthy. The harvest of the sweet potato crop was the best ever if you consider the harvest of potatoes and gold together. Getting the new bicycle was really great but he figured that learning more about Soapstone Cave probably was the greatest thing to happen to him this year.

He knew there was even more to learn about the whole Eckerberger Mountain and he couldn't wait for the next chance to explore it. He felt as though he had a lot to be thankful for this Thanksgiving season.

It had been a busy week and Harley was beginning to feel pretty drowsy after his Saturday night bath. He probably would just forget about listening to the 'Grand Ole Opera' and go on to bed. Just a few moments after his head touched the pillow he was fast asleep.

Harley began to dream about the cave and the lost Indian tribe. It was as if he was right there with Chief Gold Tooth and his people. He heard the chief tell the braves to gather all the men around the campfire for a powwow. That was what the gathering was called and it was where all the major decisions were made. The Indians began to discuss Harley Earle's fate. Some wanted him to stay and become one of them and others wanted to scalp him.

After much talk and arguing, the chief told Harley that they had decided that he could stay with them and marry his daughter if he wanted to. He would somehow have to come up with two mules to pay for her. Harley wanted to know what would be his other choices and the chief told him he would have to promise to bring back two sacks of salt. They had none and they needed some to help preserve their meat for the winter. Salt was very valuable and the Yankees had stopped letting any be shipped to the South. He promised that if they would let him go that he would bring the salt back when he could find some.

At daylight the next morning, Harley slipped out of the camp and headed back up the trail towards Soapstone Cave where the Jessie James Gang was holed up. When Harley was nearing the robber's camp, he decided to climb a big oak tree and try to see just where he was in relation to the valley below. As he reached near the top of the huge tree he could see the whole Mt. Hope Valley. Even though the Yankees had burned and destroyed about everything, it was still a beautiful sight. There was a huge plantation at the base of the mountain.

The Yankees had left standing the big home where the owner lived. They must have used it for their campsite. It must have been at least two miles from where he was. Just looking out over the valley made him homesick, but he had to complete his present mission and that was to try his best to get into that cave.

Soon he climbed down the big tree and headed on up the trail. As soon as he got close enough to see the armed robbers camp he lay still and watched to see if they were up and around yet. He could see the horses. They looked like they were tired and hungry. There was not much for horses to eat in the mountains. He began to see some movement around the cave entrance. The gang was moving slow this morning. They looked really tired. They must have ridden a long way for their last robbery.

Harley eased through the brush until he could overhear what they were saying. It seemed there was a disagreement about which bank to rob next. He heard one of them say that he was still the leader of the gang and that they were riding to Huntsville and robbing the First Citizens Bank there. He said he had word that this was the bank that all the Yankees, that were still in the South, had their money in. He was still mad at them for the way they had stole everyone's valuables and ruined the South. The leader of the gang was later identified as the real Jessie James.

Jessie told his brother, Frank, to get everybody ready to go that they would need to get on their way. He reasoned it would take at least two days of riding to get to Huntsville. Harley heard Jessie tell Frank to have the men bury all the things and most of the money that they had stolen in the back of the cave and mount up. Harley waited in the heavy brush until the gang had cleared and then he slowly crept up the trail to the front of the cave. As he entered the cave, goose bumps appeared on his arms. It was a scary place to be in.

HARLEY GOES TO AUBURN

As Harley's dream continues, we find the robbers riding hard on through the muddy streets of Mt. Hope and then on to the Byler Road. They soon rode up on what they thought was a penitentiary. Jessie and Frank sure didn't want to spend any time there. It was what was known as the worst prison of that day. The convicts were brought here that had committed the worst of crimes and made to go into the coal mines there and dig out coal for the state's use. It was told that many of the prisoners would go into the mine to dig coal never to return to their cells. They would just disappear.

The gang decided to detour around the prison for fear that they would run into the mounted guards and their dogs. The Jessie James Gang had no idea that the Pinkerton detectives were hot on their trail. They came across the Eckerberger Mountain just a day after the robbers had left.

When the Pinkerton detectives came to Soapstone Cave, the campfire was still warm, so the lawmen quickly mounted their horses and resumed their pursuit of the crooks.

They didn't even take time to search the cave where Harley was hiding. He had heard the horses coming and thought it was the gang returning from a robbery. He had no choice but to run back into the cave as far as he could. He had managed to pick up an old torch, that had been used by the gang, as he ran. It was luck that he still had a few matches wrapped in rawhide that he carried during the war. If he went much further into the cave the torch would have to be burned. There was always a danger that rattlesnakes would be somewhere back in the cave since it was cool and damp. Snakes didn't like smoke and would crawl away from a lit torch.

Harley listened for a long time and finally decided that the lawmen had gone on in pursuit of the James Gang. After determining that it was safe he returned to the front of the cave. He knew that there must be hundreds of dollars hidden in the cave and he figured that he could put that money to use or maybe to give some of it to the preacher. His preacher was always wanting to build a new church.

Since the Yankees had almost destroyed the church, the money sure would come in handy for rebuilding it. Harley also thought that at least some of the James Gang would escape from the Pinkertons if they were captured and would hightail it back to the cave to get their hidden loot. He must hurry, find the money and get away from the mountain as fast as he could.

He also had to find two sacks of salt for his new Indian friends. He would use some of the found money to buy it. Salt was more expensive than sugar or anything else that people ate. In those days people could make sugar from a lot of things, like sweet potatoes or cane. Salt had to be mined from salt mines up north and way out west.

Of course, Harley had no idea the big trouble that the James Gang had run into in Huntsville. The Pinkertons had telegraphed a message to the marshal in Huntsville to be ready for the robbers. Mr. Pinkerton had got a tip in Russellville that Huntsville was the next town that would be robbed. As the gang rode into Huntsville the streets were almost deserted. Things appeared a little too quiet to Jessie, but he decided to go ahead with their plans to rob the bank there. Little did he know that the sheriff had deputized thirty men to help with the capture of the crooks. As the gang approached the front door of the bank, shots rang out.

The robbery was over before it got started. Three of the gang were shot and Jessie and Frank surrendered and were sent back to Kansas to stand trial. They were later sentenced to life in prison for all their robberies.

Harley found the digging in the cave to be hard and dusty work. He found two sacks of money and decided that the robbery business had not been so good. He gave up the hunt and prepared to leave the cave. As he was leaving the cave he thought he needed a souvenir besides the money from the cave. He found two soapstone rocks about the size of an egg and put them into his pockets. The rocks were white and soft. They could be cut with a knife and were used by the Indians for soap.

He was now ready to go down the mountain and try to resume his life. Harley, the soldier, began to think about all the money that he was carrying. Just what was he going to do with all of it. He knew it would not be right for him to keep the money for himself. He allowed that at least half of it should go to the preacher to rebuild the damaged church. That way it would benefit everyone. The rest of it would go toward building a new schoolhouse. It would be called the Mt. Hope County Line School. It would be built at the foot of the Eckerberger Mountain. He was not sure what he would do next, but he had heard that there was a new college that had started up down at Auburn, Alabama. Men went there to learn how to be better farmers. He believed that he might just go down there and give it a try.

HARLEY MAKES MOLASSES

There was something in his dream that caused him to wake up. He thought it must have been the word, Auburn. Harley hurriedly ate his lunch and resumed his cotton picking. He knew this was most likely the last day he would get to 'scrap' cotton this year. The weather was predicted to change tomorrow and probably rain. Also, it was the last day the cotton buyers would be at Mr. Neal's Mt. Hope gin to buy the last of the crop.

Harley had sacked up what amounted to two hundred and twenty pounds. At ten cents per pound he would have $22.00 coming to him. That would just about pay for the metal detector that he would order from the catalogue. He just knew there was more gold buried somewhere around his daddy's farm and it needed to be found.

Harley had almost forgotten that next week was molasses week. This was the week that the sugar cane had to be cut and taken to the mill to be squeezed into juice and then cooked into molasses. Arnold and his brother came with their dad to help during molasses week. Usually the boys were able to get out of school for three days to help with cutting the cane. They would be allowed to make up the schoolwork later.

On Sunday the two families would get together after church service and have the Thanksgiving leftovers and that evening prepare everything for the next week's big event. There were about ten long blade knives to be sharpened to cut the cane with. The mill was over at the big spring on Mr. Jimmy D's farm. It was close to Muck City. There were about ten families that made their molasses there each year. The mill was under a big tin shed. There was a huge fireplace and chimney at one end of it. A block platform was made to connect to the fireplace and chimney. Then a long pan, maybe fifteen feet long and six feet wide, was placed on top of the blocks. Hickory wood would be placed under the pan and then when the juice was poured into it, the fire was started.

As the juice slowly traveled down the pan it would get hot and bubble up and look like golden foam. By the time it got to the end of the copper-cooking pan it would run out into a big tub. It would then be dipped and poured into one-gallon cans. Most of the time one acre of sugar cane would make 100 gallons of molasses.

The cane cutting was a dangerous business. The knives were very sharp and Harley almost cut his finger off when he was daydreaming about Soapstone Cave. He was looking forward to getting their load of cane to the mill so much that he forgot his cut and bleeding finger. He knew his mama would already be at the mill with a big picnic basket full of fried chicken, stuffed eggs, a bowl of purple hull peas, potato salad and cornbread. Harley would remember those picnic lunches at the syrup mill for the rest of his life.

The stalks of cane were unloaded and piled high beside the mill. Harley and Arnold pushed the cane in between the two metal rollers and the juice would run down into a funnel and then into a tray that went to the cooking pan. Even old Tom and Ella helped. They went round and round pulling a gear that made the rollers turn. The stalks of cane were fed into the rollers and the sweet juice was squeezed out. When the week of molasses making was finally over it was time to take the full cans home. This year was a good one for Harley's family. They had made a great sweet potato crop and the cane turned out 210 gallons of molasses.

Sunday was indeed a good one for the preacher. Harley's dad loaded up ten gallons of molasses and a big tow sack of sweet potatoes for him. Arnold's dad also brought the preacher some molasses. They figured the preacher was under paid and this would help out some with his grocery bill. Anyway, Arnold brought his bicycle and went home with Harley after church.

After dinner, Harley asked his daddy if they could ride their bikes up the road toward the mountain. This would allow his mama and daddy to get a little rest after such a hard week. The molasses week was always looked forward to but it was the hardest work they would all do during the year.

The boys were told to be back by five o'clock because Arnold's dad was going to be at Mr. Jim-So's store to pick him up. Harley had told Arnold a little about Soapstone Cave, maybe just enough to get him interested in helping to find it. They could hardly wait to get on their bicycles and be on their way. Harley was eager to show off his new bicycle to Arnold.

He wished that the horn that he had ordered would come in soon. It would fit right in the middle of the handlebars. Saddlebags would be the next thing he would order when he got the metal detector paid for.

As the boys neared the foot of the mountain they began to look for a place to hide their bikes. When the bicycles were hidden from sight of the road, they looked up toward the mountain. Harley still thought he could see a little curl of smoke in the far off distance. Who could be up there and what would they be doing? After thinking about the smoke and Soapstone Cave for a little while, Harley reasoned that he really didn't need to involve Arnold with anything to do with the Eckerberger Mountain. He told Arnold that it would be best to ride on back home because his dad would be waiting on him at Mr. Jim-So's store.

THE METAL DETECTOR

Arnold said that he guessed he would continue on with the climb that his dad could wait on him a little while if he was late getting to the store. Last Saturday night's dream about the Jessie James Gang kept coming back to Harley as he and Arnold started the climb on up toward Soapstone Cave. He was somewhat sad that the Harley of his dreams was leaving the mountain and planned to go to Auburn. He decided that he would have to do all the exploring himself and not depend on his dreams to answer his many questions about Soapstone Cave and Eckerberger Mountain.

The dreams he had this past Saturday night about the Jessie James Gang hiding the treasure in the cave was too real for him to not look for some of it himself. He believed his dream about the James Gang getting captured in Huntsville because he had read about that story in his history class. There just had to be more of that treasure in that cave than the two sacks of money that was found in the dream. There were probably a lot of gold coins somewhere up there and he was going to find them. How he wished that his metal detector would hurry up and come in from the catalogue company.

Arnold thought the climb was fun for a while but soon gave out and wanted to turn back. Harley pointed to the big birch tree that he had slept under the first time he had climbed the mountain. He was determined to go on up the mountain further this trip. He urged Arnold on. Arnold was encouraged to go on when he was told that when they got over the next hill that it would be downhill for a while. When they got to the top of the hill they could see for maybe a mile further on up the mountain. There was that curl of smoke again. Harley could not figure where smoke was coming from except that it was from the backside of the mountain. He realized that he and Arnold would never be able to go to the smoke that evening. They had already been gone two hours and it would take about that long to get back home. Arnold thought it was a good idea to turn back now. He definitely was not into mountain climbing.

When they got back to their bicycles there was a note on one of them that said, "stay off the mountain." Harley begged Arnold not to tell their folks about the note. He knew it would take more than a note to scare him off that mountain.

The next week at school was one of the longest weeks that Harley could remember. There was one good thing about the week. His metal detector came in the mail. Mr. Arthur, the mailman, brought it to the house when he came with the mail on Friday. He said he was afraid to leave it hanging on the mailbox because something might happen to what ever it was. He really just wanted to know what it was himself. Harley had just got home from school and was glad to open the package and show off the new gadget. The big problem was that it would not work on nails, pennies, jar lids or anything else. He decided he would read the instructions. He quickly found that it had to have batteries to make it work. It only needed two batteries and they would cost just fifty cents. He told his mom that Mr. Jim-So had batteries at his store and he wanted to ride his bike down there to get some. He went to his piggy bank and fished out two quarters and away he went to Mr. Jim-So's store. The store was only about one half mile from Harley's house, so he was there and back in just few minuets. When the batteries were installed he headed for the back yard and the sweet potato patch. He held the detector close to the ground as he walked over the field.

Pretty soon the gadget began to make a loud sound. Harley knew he had hit it rich. As soon as he could run to the barn and get a shovel he was back digging like crazy. About a foot down he struck something. Wouldn't you guess? It was an old horseshoe. Well it proved the thing did work.

On he went with the detector. He held it close to the ground. The alarm sounded again. Harley dug faster. This time it was an old water well bucket. Harley was still excited. About that time he heard his daddy call for him to come on to the house. It was time to do the chores. Harley hated to stop the search now but he knew he had to stay on the good side of his dad in order for him to agree to something that he wanted to do on Saturday.

Soon the chores were all done and it was suppertime. Too bad the metal detector didn't have lights with it. He had some mechanizing to do on his bicycle. He needed to fix something on it to attach the metal detector to. He had to be able to take it with him when he rode to the foot of Eckerberger Mountain this Saturday.

He couldn't decide which to do first. Should he investigate the curl of smoke or should he go to Soapstone Cave first? He would have to decide before Saturday, that is if his father did allow him to take the day off. He knew it would take the whole day for him to explore Soapstone Cave and look for the curl of smoke.

Harley and the
Bicycle Thieves

HARLEY AND THE
BICYCLE THIEVES

Saturday finally came. Harley Earle had convinced his dad that he could take the metal detector to the foot of the mountain where the Union troops camped during the Battle of Mt. Hope. There must be hundreds of musket rifle balls and old cannon balls just under the ground. If he found any they would bring a good price at the big flea market next month. Well his dad fell for Harley's story and told him that he could go to the foot of the mountain if he would promise to not go any further. Harley quickly agreed to his dad's terms.

He had swapped his baseball for a basket to put on the front of his bike with Harold, a friend that seemed to always have what a person needed when they were in a tight. Anyway it was just the thing to put his lunch sack in. He used some wire to tie a bottle of water on the side of his bike. By the time he got the metal detector attached to the bicycle, he looked like the old beggar that came through Mt. Hope one summer.

On this trip he decided that he would ride or push the bike up the side of the mountain as far as he could. The big birch tree would be a good place to stop and unload his lunch and detector. He would then find a place to hide his bicycle. There was a thicket of plum trees and some big rocks that would do for a hiding place. With all that done, he was ready for the next hike up the Eckerberger Mountain. He couldn't help but wonder if someone was watching him.

Why would anyone want him to stay away from the mountain?

This was the moment he had dreaded. Which path should he take? Should he investigate the place where the curl of smoke came from or should he go on to find Soapstone Cave? The smoke meant that there was someone that was alive up there. If someone was that far back in the mountains, it just meant one thing. They were hiding from something or someone. He had heard that there was some stealing going on around Mt. Hope. He heard at school that there were two bicycles stolen from different homes in the neighboring community of Landersville last week. He didn't think much about it at the time. Mr. Gene had also had some trouble at his farm. He always cured out the best country ham in the whole county. Someone had broken into his smokehouse and took three big hams and some sacks of sausage. None of this had anything to do with the smoke on the mountain as far as Harley could tell.

On he went. Up one hill and down the other he went. Finally, he came upon another trail. This trail was coming from a different direction. It was real smooth and looked like it had been traveled on with tires like those on his wheelbarrow. These two trails came together into one larger path. It really was now a small road. The only thing was that it didn't have any horse tracks on it. Nor did it have any footprints on it. The smooth road made his load seem lighter and that was good.

The road curved around a big group of boulders and trees. As Harley got almost to the big rocks, he almost fainted. He heard music playing. This scared the living daylights out of him. Who was playing the harmonica way up here on Eckerberger Mountain? He thought that he had come this far he may as well go ahead and see what was going on. As he crept on toward the music, he thought his heart would jump out of his chest. He thought that someone would hear his heart beat if he got any closer.

As he crawled on a little further, he began to see some movement in a clearing about 200 feet ahead. He had to see more. He left the trail and crawled through the woods to get closer. There were five men in the camp. It looked like they had been cooking over a campfire. That was where the curl of smoke had been coming from. The tent was made from tree limbs and looked like it was covered by deer hides. The biggest surprise of all was what he saw over to one side of the camp. There were at least sixteen bicycles, all lined up between two trees. He knew right away that he had run smack into the Dufus McGee Gang. They were known far and wide as the bicycle thieves. What was he going to do now?

HARLEY FINDS THE BEAR SKIN

There were about a half dozen things Harley must consider about the situation that he was in. He realized that he could not let the bicycle crooks know that he knew where they were. Another thing he knew was that he couldn't let his daddy nor anyone else know about the gang. He knew if anyone knew about the gang, then the law would come and perhaps destroy his chance to explore Soapstone Cave.

He did not want the gang to get away, but what should he do. He knew one thing for sure and that was that he sure didn't want them to steal his bicycle. He knew that the very first thing he was going to do on Monday was to take a dozen eggs to Mr. Jim-So's store and swap them for a lock to put on his bike. But what was he going to do right now? That was his first concern.

He started to crawl back to the trail that the Dufus McGee Gang had made and then try to get back to the main path that would take him to Soapstone Cave. From the amount of music and singing he was hearing he figured that the crooks must be celebrating a big robbery that they had pulled. He promised himself that as soon as he explored Soapstone Cave and uncovered the treasure, then he would alert Mr. Franklin. He was the kind of sheriff that made crooks shiver when they heard his name.

As he made his way back toward the main path he began to hear some strange sounds. They seemed to be coming from the direction where he thought Soapstone Cave was located. His heart was beating fast now. He began to think about the stories he had heard about bears and black leopards living on the Eckerberger Mountain. He needed to hurry on if he was to get to the cave today.

As he approached the trail that he assumed was the one to the cave, his stomach growled and that was his signal to take a break and eat his lunch. While eating, he noticed a new footprint that was not there when he passed by before. What did this mean? Did someone else know about the cave? He sort of lost his appetite when he saw the footprint. Again, he had to make another major decision. Should he go on or should he head for his bicycle?

Wait! He heard more noise. Harley jumped behind some bushes. He almost stopped breathing as he tried to cover himself and his metal detector with some leaves. Down the cave trail, he could see some movement. He burrowed deeper into the leaves.

He could now hear footsteps. He thought that his heart stopped or at least skipped some beats. As the sounds got closer, Harley peeped out from the bed of leaves enough to see who or what was coming down the trail. It was a young Indian about his own age and size. He had a bow and arrow and it looked like he had two squirrels hanging from his belt.

The dreams came back to Harley. All the dreams about there being a lost tribe of Indians from the "Trail of Tears" in the mountains must have been true. This Indian boy must be from that lost tribe. Harley remained hidden in the leaves until the young brave had gone on down the side of the mountain in pursuit of more squirrels. That was a close call.

He had no idea if the boy could speak his language or whether or not he might shoot him with his arrows. This mountain was getting too crowded. He only hoped that he could find the cave and treasure before too many more people showed up.

The mountain was now quiet as far as Harley could tell. The Dufus McGee Gang was at least a mile back around the mountain and the young hunter was probably back to where he lived. Harley would really like to make friends with him sometime later but not right now. Harley just had to get on toward the cave. He was getting close, he just knew it. When he came upon what looked like a pile of black hair, his heart began again to beat faster. This must be the old bear hide that had been stretched over the tree limbs to scare off anyone that came along the trail many years ago.

In any case, Harley knew that Soapstone Cave was now very near. The only thing that started to worry him now was that he would have to start back towards home now in order to get there before chore time. The next time he would make it all the way to Soapstone Cave.

Mules, Cows, Pigs and Buried Treasure

MULES, COWS, PIGS, AND
BURIED TREASURE

The bicycle was still hidden in the brush when Harley came down from the mountain. He was a little afraid it would not be there. A huge lump came up in his throat as he reached for the handlebars. There was another note tied to the seat.

The note said "last warning, do not go up the mountain again." There had been too many surprises for Harley today. He decided once again to go to Jesus for some help. This time he just asked for Jesus to give him protection from who ever was writing the notes and from the Dufus McGee Gang, the Indians, and anyone else that did not want him on Eckerberger Mountain. Oh yes, he said, Jesus please help me to not tell any more whoppers to my daddy.

It seemed that the wheels would not turn fast enough as he peddled toward home. It would be a long time before he was ready to go back up the mountain and to Soapstone Cave. He thought that he would just find all the buried silver and gold around the farm. He figured he could even hire himself out to his neighbors and find the buried money on their farms. He could make a fortune with his new metal detector.

Old Tom and Ella were glad to see Harley. They pawed their feet and nickered when he came to the barn. It was time for their twenty-four ears of corn. As he fed the mules, Harley began to wonder why he had not tried to ride the mules. It would be a faster way to get up the mountain than climbing it on his own feet.

The cows were glad to see Harley also. They liked the cottonseed meal and crushed corn that they ate while they were being milked. The pigs didn't know what was ahead or they wouldn't have been so eager to eat as much. They would nearly knock Harley down as he emptied the leftovers from the kitchen into their trough. In addition to the bucket full of leftovers the pigs would get all the ears of corn that they could eat. The three pigs were being fattened up to be slaughtered. The meat from the pigs would last the family most of the year.

As Harley was feeding the pigs, he realized that next Saturday was the second Saturday after Thanksgiving. That was the day that several families in the community would gather with their fattened pigs at Mr. Glenn's cotton gin. The hogs would be slaughtered, cleaned and cut up into pork chops, ham, bacon and sausage. When the cuts of meat were taken back to the different farms, some of it would need to be "salted down." When the meat was rubbed down with salt, it would be buried in the saltbox and covered with the rest of the salt. This would preserve the meat for months. The process could only take place when the weather was cold. Next Saturday would be a busy day. Harley had to put the mountain climbing aside for a while.

Meanwhile, the Saturday night bath, some popcorn and a time of listening to the Grand Ole Opry, would finish out the week for Harley. As he lay down he began to wonder how many miles it was to Auburn. He had overheard his F.F.A. teacher talking last week about what a great place it was. Harley lay awake for hours wondering about what he would do when he finally finished high school. Would he be like the Harley in his dreams and want to go off to that school in Auburn?

Finally he fell asleep and as usual he started to dream, only this time his dream was not about Eckerberger Mountain. It was about gold. A dream about gold was not so surprising since this was the second most important thing he thought about, right after Soapstone Cave.

Tonight, Harley's dream started at the spring, down back of the barn. He had his metal detector and was holding it close to the ground just above where the water comes out around a big rock. Nothing there, not even a little buzz from the detector.

Harley thought that the family who lived in the old house during the big war had a lot of money. He figured that they buried their money somewhere close to the house when they heard that the Yankees were coming.

As he moved up the Tannyard Creek he began to hear a little buzzing from the detector. He went on a little further. The buzzing became a lot louder. Back to the barn he went to get a shovel. Soon he was back and digging like crazy. About two feet down he struck something hard. It must be some kind of buried treasure.

He continued to dig and clear away some rocks from what looked like a metal chest or trunk. After much tugging and pulling, the trunk finally came out of the ground. The chest was made of metal and poplar wood and had not rotted while in the ground. It also had a big lock that kept it from being opened. Back to the barn to get a hammer to break the lock, he went. A few licks and the lock flew apart. Now to open the trunk.

About that time his daddy gave Harley a big shake and told him to get up and eat breakfast that it would soon be time for church.

81

Harley and the Preacher's Daughter

HARLEY AND THE
PREACHER'S DAUGHTER

When Bro. Ben resigned the church, the deacons had to find a new preacher. Harley guessed that the search team told the new man that the last preacher got rid of all the demons and left, figuring that his work was done there. The preacher that accepted the call to the church and was soon living in Mt. Hope.

He had a wife and a daughter and the girl caught Harley's eye as soon as he saw her. He wanted to make a good impression on her the very first Sunday they were at his church. Little did he know what Arnold had in mind as far as welcoming her to their church.

When the opening assembly song was over, everyone went to their Sunday school class. On the way to their class, Arnold began to whisper to Harley about the plan he had for livening the service up a bit. Harley was shocked. He knew the new girl would be the one that Arnold played his trick on, but what could he do? He didn't know of a single girl, much less a preacher's daughter, that liked frogs.

Arnold sat next to the new girl. This didn't bother Harley at all because his cousin was as ugly as a frog himself. He knew girls always looked for good looking, strong and muscled up guys. Arnold was not gifted in any of those areas. He guessed that this had a lot to do with Arnold always wanting to play pranks on people. He liked the extra attention he got from playing these tricks, even though he always got a whipping when his dad found out about them.

Arnold began to look the girl over to see just which of her pockets he would put the frog in. He finally decided that the best time to deposit the frog in her pocket was when the class was over and they were walking back to the main building for the preaching service. Harley was so nervous during the Sunday school class that he hardly knew anything the teacher said.

Sure enough, Arnold was walking right next to the new girl, whose name he had learned was Rachel. Arnold tried to get Harley to come on up and walk with the group. This was not to be. There was going to be a lot of space between him and the girl when she found the frog in her pocket. Before they went into the preaching room, Arnold slowed down and waited on Harley. As he caught up to Arnold he was told that the frog had been properly placed in Rachel's coat pocket. That did it for Harley. He knew he was not going to sit next to Arnold during preaching.

After what the two had done with the cats, people would just automatically point the finger at them. The new girl would know right away that it was Arnold because he was the only boy that had been close to her the whole day and that no girl would do such a thing.

When he saw his mama and daddy start to their seats he made a point to be right there with them. In fact he sat between them. It was a little cool in the church that morning and most people kept their coat on during the service. When he looked across the church he saw that Rachel still had hers on. He only hoped that her hands didn't get cold. But they did. Just about the time that her dad, the preacher, was into his sermon pretty good, it happened.

We all remember the passage in the bible that talked about the plagues that God sent on the pharaoh's land. The new preacher was telling the church that sometimes we are given warnings when we are not doing right. He related about how God told the pharaoh that if he didn't let his people go that he would send a plague of frogs upon his land and cause a lot of confusion to come to his people. About that time, Rachel's hands got cold. She shoved her hands down into what was normally warm pockets. Instead of a warm pocket, she felt the cold slimy frog. She jerked the frog out of her coat and threw it toward the pulpit.

The new preacher didn't know where the frog came from, but he thought that it was a sign that Harley's church people needed a lot more straightening out. He told them that he had been sent there by the Lord to do just that and that if it took a long time to do it, he would stay until the job was done.

It was a relief to Harley Earle to hear him say that he was going to be there for a long time. He wondered if Rachel had ever heard of that college at Auburn, Alabama.

HARLEY CLEANS THE STOVE PIPE

Arnold and Harley had dodged a bullet. Both boys sat far away from Rachel when the frog made it's appearance. The church people didn't really know who to blame for the incident. Some even thought it was Rachel's idea to pull the stunt. In any case, since it was the new preacher's first Sunday, most chose to just overlook what had happened. Arnold chuckled to himself and Harley just breathed a sigh of relief.

The parents of the two boys often shared Sunday lunch with each other. This Sunday was one of those days. Sunday evenings were always fun but sometimes the pranks that Arnold and Harley pulled were pretty risky. The were lucky to not get into trouble with the frog trick.

After lunch the two boys sneaked away from the house and finally got to have a big laugh about what had happened at church this morning. They really wondered what Rachel thought about it. They guessed they would hear from her next Sunday when they went to class. Harley knew one thing for sure and that was that he was not going to take any blame for what had happened. His aim was to become a friend to Rachel. A very close friend. He even hoped his folks would invite the preacher and his family to have Sunday lunch with them sometime.

The men came outside and sat on the front porch. Harley heard his dad talking about his wood fired kitchen stove. It was not heating up like it was supposed to. He reckoned the stovepipe must be clogged up with soot that had collected over the years. He would have to soon get a ladder and get up on the roof and look down the pipe to see if it was about stopped up.

Overhearing this caused Harley to think of a way to help his daddy out. He could get the stovepipe unstopped and have fun at the same time. Harley told Arnold to come with him. They went to the barn and got some long pieces of string that the bales of hay were tied with. This time Arnold was puzzled about what they were going to do, especially when he was told by Harley to catch the big tom cat.

After getting the string and the big cat Harley got the long ladder. They went back towards the house very quietly. They knew the men were on the front porch and the women were in the front room where the quilting table was set up. Arnold was told to go into the kitchen and take the top cover off the stove and catch the cat when he slowly let him down the pipe with the string. He said to catch the cat and take him outside. Harley knew that the cat would be kicking and clawing as he was let down the stovepipe. This would clear out all the smut that had collected in it over the past years. The plan seemed to be working pretty good until the cat reached the bottom of the pipe. When 'old tom' got to that point the string that was tied to his hind leg broke and away he ran. Arnold could not catch him. Around and around the kitchen the cat and Arnold ran, strewing smut, ashes and soot all over the room.

Harley knew something was wrong when he pulled up the string and nothing was on the other end. He climbed down the ladder and went inside the house. He didn't recognize Arnold. The person in the kitchen was covered in black smut and cat fur. The cat ran out of the kitchen when Harley came in and has not been seen since.

All the hollering and meowing had brought the boys parents to the kitchen. They were speechless. Harley was white as a sheet and Arnold was as black as midnight. The boys wished that they were somewhere safe, like in jail or prison where their parents could not punish them.

After a lot of moping and sweeping, things finally settled down. The kitchen floor was as clean as they could get it but it still had a sort of gray look. The boys? Well, they were still so scared of what was going to happen to them that they could hardly talk. Arnold told Harley that he was afraid his ma and pa would send him to reform school and Harley feared that he would be placed in an orphans home. The parents, following what they had been taught in church, decided not to act in haste and pray about what punishment to hand out to the two.

HARLEY DREAMS ABOUT ITASCA

Christmas holidays started on Monday the day after the stovepipe cleaning episode. There would be no school for two whole weeks. Harley's daddy and his mama debated about what to do about their son's punishment for several hours. They finally came to the conclusion that Harley would be confined to the house except for the time he would be outside doing his chores. On the surface that didn't seem so bad except that they knew how much Harley liked to be outside to explore the area around their home and the mountains. He would surely miss going treasure hunting with his new metal detector.

Monday was just plain terrible for Harley. He even looked forward to going to the barn to milk the cows. When it was time to bring in the stove wood he would bring only half what he had been bringing in before. This would mean that he would have to make twice the trips to bring in the same amount of wood. He even over- filled the wood box. He could at least listen to the radio when 'The Lone Ranger' came on. It was chores, supper, radio and then to bed. He decided he would never do anything bad again, or at least he would not get caught if he did.

Monday had been really tough on Harley. Maybe Tuesday would be better. He was allowed to go to the mailbox after Mr. Arthur, the mailman, delivered the mail. He had been looking for a package for a few days. His cousin in Texas always sent him a big box of clothes that he had outgrown during the year.

He was really happy to hear the mailman blow his horn today. This meant that the mail he had for the family was too big for the mailbox. He figured the package that he was looking for had come in today's mail. Sure enough, Mr. Arthur had a huge box for him. It was even addressed to him. The return label had his Uncle Rube's Itasca, Texas, address on it. He couldn't wait to get inside and see what was in it.

The first thing he pulled from the box was a pair of Levi's. Harley wanted to try them on, even before he looked at the other things in the box. There were several western shirts, a leather belt, more pants. He couldn't believe what was near the bottom of the box. It was a coat that was lined with sheep's wool. There was no way wind could get through this coat. Harley hollered when he saw what was in the bottom of the box. They were the prettiest western boots he had ever seen. He couldn't wait to try them on. When he put his foot in the first boot he felt something in it. It was a note. The note said, "Hope the clothes fit. Dan outgrew them. Come to Texas to see us when you can. Love, Uncle Rube and Aunt Alpha."

Harley was glad that he was at home when the mail ran this day. He spent the rest of the day trying on the clothes that cousin Danny had outgrown. When school started back he would wear his new western clothes and boots the first day.

This had been a great day, especially since he was in time out or house detention. After he hurriedly finished his chores he tried on everything again. He ate his supper in a hurry and listened to the radio for a little while. The program was called "The F.B.I. In Action." He admired the men of the F.B.I. He thought someday that he may join up with them.

Darkness came early in December and Harley got sleepy when it got dark. He never argued with his daddy about going to bed. He guessed he was just a sleepy head. In the back of his mind he thought he may even have a good dream tonight since he had enjoyed the day so much.

Sure enough, Harley Earle's dream machine started right up. This dream was a little different. Something about the day probably caused him to dream this one. Well, anyway Harley dreamed he was about twenty years old and was ready to go out in the world and earn lots of money. He dreamed that there were no jobs that he could get. He decided to jump on the freight train that passed through Russellville and head out west. He had heard that there were plenty of jobs out in Texas.

When the train slowed down at the station in Russellville, he jumped into the first boxcar that had open doors. As the train began to pull out from the train station, he heard noises over in one corner of the car. It was dark but he could see the outline of two hobos. They looked like they had been on the train for a long time. They had beards and wore ragged clothes. He clutched his small suitcase. It only had one change of clothes in it but he sure didn't want to lose what little he had.

The train blew a long lonesome whistle as it pulled away from the station in Russellville. The train stopped and started many times before it arrived in Memphis. More hobos got into the boxcar as it slowed down.

Harley decided to get off the train. He was hungry and he thought he could get a hamburger and a grape drink before the train pulled out again. The hamburger stand was not far from the boxcar. Harley ordered one hamburger and a drink and gave the cashier a quarter. He decided that he better eat the burger before getting back in the boxcar. The hobos looked pretty hungry and they might want a share of it.

He heard the conductor call out from up front. The call was for all aboard for Waco, Texas. This would be a long ride, probably about two days. The train would stop about every hundred miles and some hobos would get off and others would get on. Usually there would be time to get something to eat and drink. Harley would sure be glad when the train crossed the Texas state line.

When the train pulled into Waco Texas it was close to midnight. There was no hamburger stand open at that time, so Harley just had to wait in the train station until daylight when the cafe opened. While he was eating, he asked the cook where was the best place to find work around there. He was told that there was a lot going on around Itasca, Texas. This was about thirty or forty miles on up the road.

Catching a ride with a man hauling a load of turnips to Fort Worth was a real stroke of luck. He told the driver to let him off when he passed through Itasca. When he arrived in the bustling little Texas town he felt as though he had found the answer to his prayers.

As he walked around the town, he saw a few signs in the window that said, "Help Wanted." He soon came to the post office. There was a sign that said to apply here for work. Harley dreamed that this was where he wanted to start his career. He filled out some papers and the man behind the office window looked them over and said, "Come on in son, you are hired."

As the sun came up, Harley woke up. He was rested and happy. He thought that someday he would grow up and visit that little town called Itasca.

Harley Impresses

Rachel

HARLEY IMPRESSES RACHEL

As Harley lay in bed he began to remember hearing about how his Uncle Rube had left the dusty cotton fields in Mississippi to go west to make his fortune. He had heard that his Uncle wrote back to his brothers and encouraged them to also make the move. Harley also had heard that Uncle Rube had found a pretty red headed Texas girlfriend. That could have been the reason for liking Texas so much Having all this information and getting the package yesterday must have had a lot to do with his dream last night.

The smell of country ham cooking was enough to make Harley decide to get out of bed. Country ham and red eye gravy with some pear preserves was his favorite breakfast. The next few days were going to be a real struggle. All he could do was just plan his next climb up the mountain. He decided that it would be a good idea to do everything that his mama and daddy wanted him to do, at least for the rest of this week. He would have a whole week left of Christmas vacation to do some things that he wanted to do, mainly, climbing Eckerberger Mountain.

Many times during the next three days, Harley went to the big clock on the mantel and checked to see if it was running or if it needed to be wound up. His mama told him to stop the winding because he would break the winding spring. He remembered an old saying that there was a silver lining in every cloud. Harley reasoned that the silver lining to this week was that it would soon be Sunday.

Sundays had taken a whole new meaning to him since Rachel had joined their church. He had to figure out a way to impress her in a very positive way. On Saturday night Harley's week got a big boost. He overheard his daddy ask his mama if she thought she could fix dinner for the preacher and his family this Sunday. Harley held his breath until his mama answered that she guessed it would be okay and that she could cook turkey and dressing.

Harley began to make plans for the Sunday evening that Rachel would be at their house. He didn't know if she was a tomboy or just a girlie girl. He hoped that she was more of a tomboy. He didn't know much about how to impress a girlie girl. The best thing he could come up with was to show her his metal detector.

Sunday school went pretty smooth except that Rachel got up and moved when Arnold sat down by her. You could tell that she knew who put the frog in her pocket. Arnold just sat by himself and sulked. Harley guessed that Arnold would learn his lesson by Rachel giving him the cold shoulder. He doubted that his cousin would ever put a frog in anyone else's pocket, especially in a girl's pocket.

The lesson went very good and the teacher, Miss Christine, told the class that she was very proud of them. It was good for Rachel to hear that she was in a good group of boys and girls.

Soon, the preacher was pounding his fist on the pulpit and waving his arms in the air while all the time, preaching the word. His sermon centered on treasures on earth, compared to the treasures in heaven. He reasoned that the treasures we lay up here on earth will not in any way compare with those in heaven. Harley listened very close to what he was preaching. He hoped he would not hear anything that would put a damper on what was planned for this afternoon.

After the sermon was over the preacher and his family got in their car and followed Harley's family to their house. When they arrived the women went inside and the men sat on the porch. The weather was unusually warm for December. Before too long the men were called to come on in to dinner. Harley's daddy said that since the preacher was paid to preach and pray, would he please pray over the food. Every one but Harley Earle ate all that was on their plates. He was just too nervous to eat. It was also hard for him to eat with one hand. Impressing Rachel was important so he tried to use all the manners he knew about.

After the desert was served and everyone was finished, it was now time for Harley to make his move. He finally got up the nerve to ask Rachel if she would like to see his metal detector. She surprised him by saying she would and that she had always wanted one for herself. She said that a lot of churches had big cracks in the floors and that sometimes the offering plate got turned over and some of the coins fell through the cracks. She thought if she had a detector she could find some of them.

The two went outside with the detector and began to move it over the dirt around the front yard. When they got close to the mailbox the buzzing started. After getting the shovel and rake, the digging started. First it was a dime, then a penny and the buzzing stopped. Finding eleven cents was the starting of a good relationship. Harley had a smile as big as a wave on a slop bucket. The rest of the evening was a lot of fun. When the buzzing started they could hardly wait to dig up what treasure they had found. The treasures that they found that evening included the eleven cents, one musket rifle ball, two horseshoes, three jar lids and part of an old knife. This was a great start for the two treasure hunters. They both agreed that these treasures surely would not measure up to the treasures they would get in heaven.

WHAT IS THE MATTER WITH HARLEY EARLE?

Harley Earle hated to see this Sunday evening come to an end. He felt that he now had a new friend. It was really a stroke of luck that Rachel liked using his metal detector. He figured she must be one in a hundred when it came to a girl liking to hunt for hidden treasures. In any case, she told him that she would like to go treasure hunting with him again sometime. She also wondered if he would sometimes loan the metal detector to her. She just knew that there would be a lot of coins under the church where her dad had last served as preacher. Harley agreed that she could borrow it sometime. He knew that there must be sacrifices sometimes in order to get on the good side of girls.

It was time for the preacher and his family to leave for their home. The church at Mt. Hope didn't hold services on Sunday night. The people there didn't think they needed as much preaching as city folks did.

It was now time for the chores to be done. Harley didn't seem to mind doing them this evening. He would have time to think about the fun that he had had all day. The only thing was, that when he was milking, he just kept on milking when his bucket was full. He also kept drawing water from the well and filling the water trough, even though it was running over. He even gave old Tom and Ella, the mules, twenty-four ears of corn each instead of twelve each. Later, when he was at the supper table, he filled his plate with turnip greens even though he never ate them before. What in the world was the matter with Harley Earle?

Harley's mama was really surprised to see him so hungry for turnip greens. She asked him, "Harley, when did you take such a liking to turnip greens?" He just then realized he had a problem in that he didn't like them at all, but he couldn't tell her that he had something or someone on his mind and just was not thinking about what he was doing. He finally decided it was best that he hold his nose and go ahead and eat them, pretending that he had liked them all along.

She wondered about his answer and doubted he would ever eat them again. Harley had no idea that girls could cause this kind of confusion in ones life.

After a while, Harley became sleepy and decided he would just go on to bed and with any luck he would dream about Soapstone Cave. He did have more trouble going to sleep than he thought he would. The thoughts about the day with Rachel and the metal detector kept him awake. When he finally did go off to sleep he didn't dream about Soapstone Cave, the metal detector, or Rachel. Instead he started to dream about the buried treasure in the trunk at the spring down behind the house.

The big lock was about rusted away, but it still took several good hits with the hammer that he had got at the barn. The lock flew off and the lid of the trunk could now be opened. The treasure was inside of a metal can. He tried to unscrew the top off the can. It was rusted on real good. Finally, he got the top off. Inside the can was what looked like the hide of a deer. It was wrapped around the treasure. He couldn't wait to get it out of the can.

As he pulled it out he scratched his arm. When the hide and treasure was out of the can he unrolled it and there it was, a sack of gold and silver coins. There was a note in the sack. He could barely read it because it had been in the trunk so long and the paper was easy to break. The note said, "This money was hid when we heard that the Yankees was a coming. If it is found it will mean that we left the country before they got here and we will be back to claim it someday." The note was signed, 'Dufus McGee and Family', April 20th, 1863.

Harley became so nervous and scared in his sleep that he almost woke up. He remembered that he had heard that the Yankees had come through the Mt. Hope Valley about that time. That meant that the money had been buried about ninety years. Surely Dufus McGee was dead by now. But what about his family?

What was he going to do with the gold and silver? After thinking about the situation for a while, Harley decided to go ahead and take the money to the barn and hide it where he always hid things that he did not want anyone to know about. He also allowed that he would write a letter to the Dufus McGee family and tell them what happened to the coins.

He would wrap the letter in the deerskin and then put it into the metal can and then into the trunk and then he would bury the trunk where he had found it. When he had hid the gold and silver in the barn he went to the house and found some writing paper and began to write the letter.

The letter started off by saying how sorry he was that they had not made it back after the war. He continued writing that he was sure that all of the family was dead and would have no use for the buried money. In the letter he stated that the money would be used wisely and that he would give ten per cent of it to the church. After finishing the letter he hurriedly took it back to the trunk and buried it.

HARLEY TAKES A NEW INTEREST IN SCHOOL

When Harley woke up the next morning it seemed that he had just laid down on the bed. He was very tired. It seemed to him like he had dug potatoes and hoed cotton all day and into the night.

He then began to remember his dream. That was why he was so tired. He must have made a 100 trips to the barn and back to the buried treasure. That was why he was so tired. He also felt a little pain on his arm. There was a long scratch on it. The scratch was like the one he got in the dream. This was a sign to him that there really was a buried treasure out there somewhere just waiting on him and his metal detector to find it.

Well, it was Monday and that meant school. His vacation time was over. As he thought back about the past two weeks, he felt that he had spent the time well. After all he believed that he had impressed Rachel, and he had learned a lot from his dreams. Christmas Day had been good. He was happy to get a new battery powered horn for his bike. Old Santa knew just what he needed. The new Barlow pocketknife was going to come in handy when he went exploring again. Probably the most useful thing he got was the flashlight his dad gave him. His dad said he could use it when he had to go feed the horses before daylight some morning. Harley already had a use figured out for the flashlight. Soapstone Cave must go far back into the mountain. He didn't want to have to use a burning torch to

101

see what was hid back in the cave. Maybe it wouldn't be too long before he could go back up the mountain and hunt for the treasure that he knew was buried there.

Breakfast was ready. While he was eating his egg and biscuit and the molasses that he had helped make during the fall, his mama reminded him that he would need to find some eggs at the barn when he came in from school. It seemed that the old hens were hiding them so they could hatch a new batch of little chicks. He sometimes would find a hen setting on a nest with ten or twelve eggs in it. The mama hen would peck and scratch anyone that tried to get her eggs. If she could set on the eggs for twenty-one days before someone found them, they would hatch out into little chickens.

Harley liked to hunt for hen nests most of the time but he had so many things on his mind to do that he hated to spend any time doing it now. Exploring Eckleburger Mountain, looking for Soapstone Cave, spying on the bicycle thieves, and hunting for gold with his metal detector was a better use of his time and much more important to him than hunting hen eggs.

Right now he had to hurry and get ready for the school bus. Uncle Gus would be blowing his bus horn in a few minuets. Harley was at the road when he heard Uncle Gus blow his horn. The bus came to a stop and Harley got on. He almost fainted when he saw Rachel sitting on the front seat. This was one of the few times that he could not talk. Where was he to sit? Should he sit across from her? Should he go to the back seat where he usually sat? He froze in his tracks. Uncle Gus said, "Harley find you a seat and we will get on down the road." Harley came out of his trance and nodded his head at Rachel and took a seat near the back. What was she doing on this bus?

As they got off the bus and walked toward the school building, he overheard Rachel tell a girl that her daddy was the new preacher at the church in Mt. hope and that they had just moved into the house just down the road from Mr.Jim-So's store. She told the girl that she was in the eighth grade and didn't know which room to go to. The girl told her to follow her and that she would be in her room. Harley was still so much in shock that he had yet to say a word to her.

When the bell rang, he and the rest of the eighth graders went to Miss June's room. Sure enough, there was Rachel sitting on the front row. That would be a safer place to sit than closer to the back. That was where Arnold sat. He was always causing trouble. Harley decided he had better not tell Arnold about his and Rachel's evening of hunting buried treasure. That would just make Arnold want to pull a prank on her that much more.

Miss June welcomed the new student to Mt. Hope School and told her what a great school it was. She mentioned that some of the most highly decorated war heroes had finished school here. It had even been the school of at least one governor of the state and that several doctors, preachers, and college professors had gone to school here. She said that it had even been the school she and her boyfriend had gone to.

It was finally lunchtime and all the eighth graders marched out to the lunchroom. He watched closely to see where Rachel was going to sit. Several girls sat at the table with her. They seemed to be getting along well, at least they giggled a lot. For some reason, Harley was glad that no boys sat at her table.

After lunch, Miss June began to give some instruction concerning writing stories. She reasoned that if she could teach her students how to write a short story that they would be better prepared to write the mid term paper. The short story would need to be only about 500 words and it should be about something they had done or always wanted to do. They could not copy the story from any book or paper. It had to be their own story. The story should be finished by the time class ended tomorrow. This really got Harley's mind to going in high gear. He had so many stories to tell that he didn't know which one to write about. He wondered what Rachel would write about.

When it came time for recess, Arnold came up to Harley and began to tell him about some of the tricks that they could pull on the new girl. Harley didn't want to appear to Arnold that he liked Rachel, so he just told him that Miss June would be looking out for her for a few days and that they had better wait until later for the tricks. He did remind Arnold that he thought Rachel already knew that he put the frog in her pocket.

The day was finally over and Uncle Gus and his bus was waiting on the riders to get aboard. Harley would be glad to get home, he had a lot to think about and a story to write. He wanted his story to be the best one in the class.

Harley and the FFA
Trip to the River

HARLEY AND THE F.F.A. TRIP TO THE RIVER

After getting off the school bus Harley wasted little time with cookies and milk. He wanted to start his short story as quick as he could. His mother thought something must be wrong with her son, because he usually put off doing his homework as long as possible. She didn't ask any questions about his sudden desire to do school work. It was a pleasant surprise to her. Harley sharpened his No. 2 lead pencil with his new Barlow knife and started right in to writing his story.

Miss June said the story was to be something that one had done or always wanted to do. That was easy for Harley. There were a lot of things that he had wished he could do.

His story started off with the title at the top of the paper. The title read, "Harley Earle And His F.F.A. Trip To The River."

Harley wrote, "I left for a week of fishing, noodling, swimming, and exploring on the great Tennessee River on June 1st, 1952. Most of the boys my age and a little older would go on the F.F.A. trip every year. Mr. Hawkins, my agriculture teacher, loved this week almost as much as the boys did. He usually sat on a certain rock by the river and fished while the rest of us did what boys usually do on a trip like that.

This was the week after school was out for the summer. Daddy said we would not start hoeing cotton for two more weeks and he guessed I could go. Naturally, Arnold was along on the trip.

The first night we all sat around a big campfire and roasted hot-dogs over the open flames. There never was a hot-dog that tasted as good as those did that night on the riverbanks of the Tennessee River.

After we ate all we could hold, we fished a while. It was too dark for cork fishing, so I just baited my hook with some chicken liver and threw it out into the river as far as I could. It sank to the bottom of the river and I just leaned back on a big rock and waited for some big fish to take it away. Well, I didn't have to wait long. I felt a big tug on my line and I gave my fishing rod a big lift upwards. I had him hooked good. When I finally got the fish in I was give out. He must have weighed ten pounds. Mr. Hawkins later said it was more like two pounds.

After showing my catch to the boys, I was ready for a hike with Arnold. He was too fidgety to fish. We climbed up the hill to the cafe to see what was going on up there. It had been about two hours since we had eaten and the hamburgers smelled too good to pass up. After two hamburgers we were full and tired, so we headed back to camp. We had found a good place to lay out our sleeping bags. It was down close to the rivers edge and away from all the noise that the others were making.

Arnold and I had never been to the river before and didn't know that the river always rose about two feet every night. The people at the Wheeler Dam always let a lot of water through the dam at night to flood the places where the mosquitoes were laying eggs. This kept them under control. Anyway, we awoke about daylight with the waves washing over us. It didn't take us long to look for somewhere else to sleep. It took two days for the sleeping bags to dry out.

The next day Mr. Hawkins told us where there was a creek that flowed into the river and that there was some good noodling there. I had never heard of noodling before. Some of the older boys knew how to noodle and I decided to go along and learn how.

The creek was about waist deep and as wide as our garden. The older boys showed me and Arnold how to do it. We are both quick learners when it comes to doing something fun. We would go to the side of the creek and feel under the water into the holes in the bank. When we found a hole in the side of the creek, we would run our arms up into it as far as we could. Sometimes there would be a catfish up in that hole. I was able to pull out three fish from their hiding places that day. Arnold was too scared to try it. He did help me clean the fish and we roasted them on a metal rod over the campfire that night. That day had turned out pretty good as far as I was concerned.

There was an island out in the river about a mile down from where out camp was located. It sure looked like it needed exploring. When me and Arnold were over at the creek, we saw where fishermen rented boats. We talked it over and decided to rent one for $2.00 per day. We told Sherman what we were going to do and he thought we ought to tell Mr. Hawkins what we were up to, but we thought he might tell us not to do it.

We got our fishing tackle box and backpack and slipped away to the boat rental place. We made the deal with the rental man and took off. As we paddled our rented boat out into the river we found that the current was much stronger that we thought it would be. This was going to be fun. We just had to sort of guide the boat and didn't have to paddle hardly any. When we got close to the banks of the island, we began to hear a lot of strange noises. It was too late to turn back now so we paddled up to the bank and tied the boat to a tree stump.

We got out of the boat with our supplies and started to hike around the island. We had only walked about 100 feet when we heard the sounds again. We didn't know whether to run back to the boat or to hunt a tree to climb. The noise stopped and we went on, this time into the wooded part of the island. There were thousands of tracks on the dirt path. None of them looked the same. That meant that there was more than one or two different animals here. After walking over a large part of the island we thought it was about time to be heading back. When we got back to the place where the boat had been tied up. The boat was gone. All that was there was the rope. It had not been tied to the boat well and the waves from the river had made the boat move around so much that it came untied. At least that was what we wanted to believe.

Me and Arnold was scared to death. It was getting close to sundown and yet, no sign of the boat. I decided to build a campfire just in case we had to stay all night on the island. The fire kept ever what it was that made the strange noises away while we waited to be rescued.

Sure enough, about dark a coast guard boat pulled up to the island. One of the guards got out of the boat and came over to our campfire. He said for us to get our gear together and he would take us back to the rest of our group. When we got in their boat we saw our boat tied to the back of theirs. The coast guard fellows gave us a pretty good tongue lashing about what we had done. Mr. Hawkins didn't think we were very smart either. He said that there were bears on that island and we were lucky they didn't eat us for supper."

Harley stopped writing his story and went to the barn to do the things. After supper, he finished his short story by writing that even though this story was made up, he still planned to go to the river with Mr. Hawkins this summer and fish and noodle and maybe even rent a boat.

INSIDE THE SOAPSTONE CAVE

After using his imagination all evening writing his story, Harley was exhausted. He was not used to using his brain so much in such a short time. As he lay down for the night, he started to think about the next day and even more about the day after tomorrow. The school would shut down that day for the new years celebration. Most of the men and boys would listen to the radio or look at that new invention called a television. They would be watching or listening to the football bowl games. Harley had something more important to do during his day off from school.

The next morning as he was getting ready for school, he wondered if he had been dreaming about all the things that had happened the day before. Would she be on the bus this morning? If she was, then he would know that it had not been a dream.

As Uncle Gus screeched the old bus to a stop in front of the house, Harley ran to get aboard. When he stepped up into the bus his heart was pounding. Sure enough, there she sat, right on the front seat. This morning instead of just nodding to her, he nodded and smiled and sat just two seats behind her. He was making progress.

When they got to Miss June's class, everyone was excited. After roll call she asked for volunteers to read their short story. No one volunteered. Harley wanted to read his but he didn't want to be first. Miss June started down the roll. By the time she got to his name everyone was about to fall asleep, because the stories were so dull. Harley's name was called and he stood up and read his story. When he was finished reading, everyone clapped for him. He was embarrassed and his face turned red but he was happy that they all liked his story.

Rachel's name was the last one to be called on, but as she arose to read her story, the bell rang. He would just have to wait to see what her story was about.

As Harley boarded the bus for home he saw that all the seats were full except the one directly behind Rachel. He had no other choice. When he sat down she turned around and said to him, "I enjoyed your short story." She also said that she thought that he may even get an 'A' for his grade. Harley told her thanks and that he was looking forward to hearing her story.

He felt that he was really making progress now. He then began to think about what he was going to do the next day since he would be out of school. There were some things more important than making a good impression on girls.

When Harley got off the bus he told Rachel bye and ran to the house. He never looked back to see if she told him bye or not. As soon as he had his cookies and milk he asked his mama if there was anything that she needed him to do. She told him that the front yard needed sweeping and that she needed some sweet potatoes brought to the house. The potatoes had been buried in and around the potato house. They always had to cover them in straw, then put a layer of dirt over the straw, and then some more straw, and then more dirt. This would keep them from freezing during the winter.

By the time he finished these two chores his daddy came in from work. He asked him the same question as he had asked his mama. This surprised Harley's daddy. He usually had to ask Harley to do the 'things'. That was short for milking, feeding the mules and filling the water trough with water. Harley's dad said, "Just go ahead and finish the barn work and I may think of something else for you to do."

Harley needed for everyone to be in a good humor when he asked about going arrowhead hunting tomorrow. Sure he would hunt for arrowheads a little but he would be spending most of the day exploring the great Eckerberger Mountain.

After supper, Harley reminded his folks that tomorrow was a holiday from school and he would like to spend some tune scouring the mountainside for arrowheads. His dad reminded him that he needed to find some more hen nests and clean out old Tom and Ella's barn stall before he went to the mountain. That wouldn't take long, maybe an hour, then he would be on his way. He decided to go on to bed while he was ahead and not give his daddy time to think of more things to do.

Harley was up early on New Year's Day. He even cleaned out the mule's stalls before his mama had breakfast ready. After he had eaten four biscuits, some deer sausages, and two fried eggs he was ready to find as many setting hens as he could and be on his way. After a while he found two nests with a total of eighteen eggs in both. With the other eggs he would normally get, that would still give them enough to sell a dozen to the rolling store when it came by on Friday.

The bicycle was loaded down with everything Harley thought he would need for his trip to the mountain. He took a good sack to put the treasure in. He just knew he would find a lot of stolen gold. If he didn't find any, he would put some arrowheads in the sack.

When he got to the foot of the mountain, he decided he would push the bike up as far as he could and then hide it. He was not going to hide it where it could be found by the 'note writer' this time. When he hid the bike and tied all his supplies and backpack across his back, he was ready for the climb. He used his metal detector as a walking stick and started up the trail to Soapstone Cave.

This trip up to the cave went a lot faster. He knew where he was going this time. After about two hours he was at the entrance of the cave. His heart was really pounding. He didn't know if it was from the climb or just the thought of going into the cave that caused it to beat so fast.

The cave still smelled of pine smoke. He lit a match to a stick and watched where the smoke went. It went into the cave. That meant that there must be an entrance at the back of the cave where the smoke would be drawn out at. He entered the cave. It was big enough for several horses to stand in.

There were long icicles made from rock hanging from the top of the cave. Some of them shined like they were made from diamonds when he shined his flashlight on them. Over to one side of the cave was a pile of rocks. They were different to any he had ever seen before. You could take one and mark on the side of the cave with it. There were several words written on the wall. One name on the wall was Jessie James. Another writing said, 'There are ghosts in this cave.' Another name on the wall was that of Dufus McGee. That name caused goose bumps to come up on Harley's arms. That meant the Dufus McGee Gang knew where Soapstone Cave was located.

After thinking about it a little while he decided that the younger McGee Gang may not know about the cave after all. The Dufus McGee that put his name on the wall was most likely the same one that had buried the trunk of coins down by the creek and that Dufus had probably been dead for fifty years.

Harley reasoned that someone before him may have been in the cave looking for treasure but none of them had a metal detector like he had. He was back in the cave far enough now that it was getting dark. He was real glad his daddy had given him the flashlight for Christmas, it was going to come in real handy now. He turned it on and kept on walking back into the cave. He could no longer see the entrance of the cave. When he turned his light off it was darker than any dark night he had ever seen.

With the light out, he sat down and listened to the stillness. Wait, what was that? It sounded like rain. He knew it was not raining outside. The sun was shining bright when he went into the cave. He turned his flashlight on and went a little further into the cave where he discovered what was making the sound.

HARLEY EXPLORES THE SOAPSTONE CAVE

Harley never thought he would ever see anything so beautiful in his life. The sound he was hearing was water dripping from the top of the cave into a big lake. The lake was about the size of a football field. When he shined his flashlight out over the water it looked like a sea of silver flakes falling. The water was as clear as new glass. He could see all the way to the bottom of the lake. There were fish swimming around the edge of the water. The only thing was that they looked like they didn't have any eyes. He guessed they didn't need any since it was so dark. They did swim away when he pitched a pebble into the water. Harley guessed they could at least hear.

There was still plenty of room to walk around the lake on one side. When he got to the end of the lake there was a stream going on back into the cave. He thought he would follow it for a while. Maybe it would lead to the back entrance of the cave. As he walked on further, the passage became narrower. He soon had to stop because he came to a place where he would have to cross the stream and it was too wide for him to jump over. It also looked to be several feet deep. He would need a long log to put across it before he could get to the other side. That would be something he could do the next time he came to Soapstone Cave.

He had explored the cave enough this trip and he decided that he had better head back toward the entrance and try using his metal detector. It seemed like it took him longer to get back to the entrance than it did to get to the water.

He started to think about Miss June's English class. He would sure be ready to write the long story that would come due at the end of the year. He had not even used the detector yet but he knew that what he had seen so far would be enough to have the class clapping their hands harder than they did when he read the short story.

He would have to change the location of the cave in that story. He didn't want anyone to even have a hint about where his Soapstone Cave was located.

On his first walk along the side of the cave with his detector, there was a buzzing sound from it. He just then realized that he had not brought a shovel with him. He would just have to dig with sticks and rocks. He would dig a few moments and have to stop and rest. He was not making much progress because the ground was rocky and very hard to dig in. When he was about a foot down he stopped and turned on the detector again. He placed it right over the hole. It buzzed a little louder.

It was now getting late in the evening and he knew he had to leave the cave in a few minuets in order to get back to his bicycle and on to his house before dark. The batteries in his flashlight were also getting weak. He had to hurry. He dug faster. Just as his flashlight went out he thought he felt something in the bottom of the hole.

More digging, this time in the dark. It was a metal box. He could tell that it had no handle on it and he couldn't get it out of the ground. What was he to do now? It was either dig a lot more and be caught on the mountain without any light or leave now. At last he had the good sense to gather up his supplies and get ready to leave. He put dirt back into the hole and covered the newly disturbed soil with rocks and left the cave.

Harley remember to put some of the arrowheads in his sack that lined the trail and soon he was down the mountain and to the hiding place of the bicycle. It was not there. Harley, once again, almost had a heart attack. He had been warned two times to not go back up the mountain. Now he had no choice, he had to tell his daddy about the Dufus McGee and the bicycle thieves.

The long walk home with all his supplies was going to be very tiring but he had to hurry because he wanted to get home before night. The thieves might still be around and he did not want to meet up with them in the dark. Just as he was nearing the bottom of the mountain, there was a lot of hollering in front of him and in behind him as well. He had been surrounded by the Dufus McGee Gang. There were three in front of him and two in back of him. They all had masks on and were riding bicycles.

The leader, whom Harley figured must be Dufus McGee the third, told Harley that this was his last warning. He was not to go into the mountain again. He would find his bicycle at the bottom of the hill. Dufus said that the mountain was his now and it had been his grandfather's since before the big Civil War. The Yankees had run them off the mountain and all the way to Arkansas, but he was back to reclaim what was his.

Harley was in no position to argue with the gang. He had to think fast. He figured that the gang was in trouble with the law so he would just share some information with them. It was information that Harley had just made up in his own mind. He asked Dufus McGee if he had seen Sheriff Franklin today? Dufus became very nervous and answered that he had not seen him and asked Harley where did he reckon the sheriff was right now? Harley said that Mr. Franklin came by the house this morning before he left for the mountain. He said he overheard the sheriff tell his daddy that there were some thieves hiding out up on the

Eckerberger Mountain and that he was going to catch them and put them in the penitentiary.

Harley told Dufus that if he saw any thieves to be sure and tell them that Sheriff Franklin was probably the toughest lawman in this part of the country and was often compared to Marshall Matt Dillon and Wyatt Earp. He also said that a lot of crooks the sheriff caught went to Kilby Prison and they were never heard of since.

For a few minutes Harley could hardly breath for the dust that all the bicycles stirred up as they left for Arkansas. Dufus had heard of the penitentiary in Montgomery and wanted no part of it. The last thing Harley heard from Dufus McGee as he peddled out of sight was for him to take care of his mountain and that he would be back when Sheriff Franklin got beat in the next election.

Harley hoped that would be a long time from now. He gathered up his backpack and metal detector and headed on down the trail to the bottom of the mountain. The bike was right where Dufus said it would be. He quickly got aboard it and peddled toward home as fast as he could. When he reached home, his mama told him that supper would be ready by the time he got the things done.

The day had not been all that he had hoped for, but all in all he had accomplished quite a lot. He had found the treasure. He had found the lake of clear water. He had found some of the soapstone rocks. He had single handed run off the Dufus McGee Gang without firing a shot. Now he was going to have a good supper of fried chicken and hot biscuits with brown gravy. What else could a boy want?

There was just one more thing that Harley Earle had to do that day. He got on his knees and asked Jesus to one more time forgive him for telling a big one to Dufus, but he just figured it was the best way to prevent bloodshed.

HARLEY SAVES THE SCHOOL

The New Year came in like a lion. On January 2nd, Harley woke up early. The wind was howling and he could hear something hitting the tin roof of their house. What was it? He opened one eye and crept over to the window. He could hardly see through it. There was something covering the outside of it. It was ice and snow.

Yesterday was such a pretty day. Harley didn't even have to wear a coat when he went to the Eckerberger Mountain. It must have been snowing for several hours because there was about six inches of the white stuff on the ground. That would be enough to keep Uncle Gus's bus at home. There would be no school today.

Harley couldn't decide whether he was sad or glad about not having school that day. For some reason he had taken on a new attitude about going to school. He looked forward to going. But on the other hand playing in the snow was a lot of fun to. He finally decided that it would be a good day. He would help his daddy do the things and then hitch old Tom up to the sled that they used to haul water from the spring and ride it all over the place. That would be real fun.

There was nothing like a big breakfast of hotcakes, butter and molasses on a snowy morning. After eating all he could hold, he and his daddy went to the barn to do the things. When they were finished, they hitched old Tom up to the sled and went for a ride. Harley told his dad that he needed to take some eggs to Mr. Jim-So's store and swap them for some batteries. The sled ride would be fun and he could get the batteries and be ready for the next trip to Soapstone Cave.

Old Tom seemed to be enjoying pulling the sled in the snow. It had been several years since the last snow, in fact it was before old Tom was born. Harley could barely remember snow covering the ground. After snow sledding for several hours old Tom was put back in the barn and Harley went on to the house. His mama had just finished making a big bowl of snow cream.

As Harley sat before the open fireplace, eating his snow cream, he began to get sleepy. He lay back on the couch and was soon fast asleep. His dream started like this.

Harley dreamed that he had better check on the money that he had hidden in the barn. It was the money that old Dufus McGee had buried in the metal box that he had dug up earlier down by the spring. He had no idea what the old gold and silver coins were worth but it was time he found out. How was he going to learn of its worth?

Finally he thought about Mr. Jimmy Langston. He was the head of the Mt. Hope Banking Company and was the most respected man in the community. Mr. Jimmy had made a lot of money and knew all about investing it in valuable things like land, cattle and gold. He would take the coins to the bank and talk with him about what they were worth.

As he was uncovering the coins, he began to wonder what he was going to do with all the money that the coins would bring. He decided he had better find out how much they were worth before he figured out how he was going to spend the money.

The sack of coins was much heavier now than he had remembered it to be when he hid it last week. That was good. The heavier the bag was, the more money the banker would pay for what was in it. It would be a long walk to the bank but he wanted to cash in on his riches quickly. It would be nice to be a rich man.

As he started the long walk to Mt. Hope, he again started to think about what he was going to do when he became rich. The first thing he thought of was a new pickup truck. He guessed walking with this heavy sack of coins was what made him think about getting a truck. Then he would buy some new boots and one of them new 'Daisy Rider B-B Guns'. It was going to be real hard to figure out how to spend all that money.

When Harley had walked about halfway to Mt. Hope, he heard a car coming up behind him. As it got closer he recognized the car as the one that Mr. Cox, the principal at Mt. Hope School, owned.

Mr. Cox pulled up to where Harley was standing and asked him if he wanted a ride. As they were riding on down the gravel road, Mr. Cox asked him if he went to school. Harley told him that he went to the little school down on county line road and that he would be coming to Mt. Hope School next year. Mr. Cox looked very sad and told Harley Earle that there would probably not be school there next year. The building had burned down and that there was no money to rebuild it.

They rode on in silence until they got to Mt. Hope. As Harley was getting out of Mr. Cox's car he asked the principal how much it would cost to build a new school-house. The principal replied that he guessed it may cost as much as $10,000 to build a new one. Harley thanked the teacher for the ride and headed for the bank.

This was the first time that Harley had ever been inside the bank at Mt. Hope. He asked the secretary if he could see Mr. Jimmy. In just a few minuets Mr. Jimmy came out of his office and asked Harley to come in. After he was seated with his sack of coins still in his hands, Mr. Jimmy asked him what he could do for him. Harley stuttered and began to tell the banker that he needed some advise about something.

Harley stood up and poured out the bag of coins on Mr. Jimmy's desk. It had been a long time since this successful man had been this excited. As he looked at the pile of gold and silver coins he asked Harley where he had gotten all the coins. Again, Harley stuttered and finally got out the words, "I found them." That would do for now, he would tell Mr. Jimmy the whole story later.

After Mr. Jimmy had looked at the coins for a while, he asked Harley if he knew how much they were worth? Harley replied that he didn't but that he would like to know their value. After counting the coins and doing a little figuring, Mr. Jimmy told Harley that they were probably worth about $10,000.

When Harley heard that $10,000 amount he immediately thought about the burned down Mt. Hope School and that it could be rebuilt for that much money. That settled it as far as Harley was concerned. The school would be rebuilt. He told Mr. Jimmy all about digging up the money and about the note that was found in the trunk. He also told him about his conversation with principal Cox and that the school would not open next year because it had burned down. Harley told the banker that since the money was not really his that he would like to see it used to build the school back. A tear rolled down the old banker's cheek. He had not known of many people in his long life that had been this generous with their money.

Harley asked Mr. Jimmy if he would see that the school board and Mr. Cox got the money to build the school. The banker said he would and so, Harley left the bank. It would be a lot easier walking home, since he no longer had the sack of heavy coins.

When Harley's daddy put a big log on the fireplace, it made a big noise. This caused Harley to wake up. After he had some more snow cream it was time for him to go out and do the things. He was glad he had a school to go to tomorrow.

HARLEY HEARS RACHEL'S SHORT STORY

The snow had melted some by the next morning. Harley was sure glad because it meant that Uncle Gus would be rumbling down the road at the regular time. School would open right on time and classes would be on schedule. This was good. Harley had several things on his mind today. First, he would be looking for Rachel to be on the front seat of the bus, second, he would be interested in hearing her short story, thirdly, he wanted to ask the principal if he knew if the school had ever burned and how did it get built back, and also, who was the principal when it burned? It would make his day if he got good answers to all of these questions. When Harley Earle got on the bus, there was the answer to his first question. Rachel was sitting on the front seat all warped up in her rabbit fur coat.

The day was starting off good. Everyone on the bus was talking about what they had done the day before. It only snowed about every four or five years and caused quite a lot of excitement when it did. Almost everyone talked about making a snowman. Harley had forgotten to do that. They talked about the carrot they used for his nose and pieces of coal for his nose and teeth. Bright colored buttons were used for his eyes and grass for his hair. Of course everyone had an old hat for his head. Some used a scarf or an old tie around his neck.

Uncle Gus barely kept the bus from slipping into the ditches but they were soon at school. As soon as the kids came off the bus they were hit with snowballs. Somehow, Arnold had beat everyone to school and recruited a bunch of his buddies to pound everyone with snowballs when they got off the buses. Arnold couldn't wait to throw one at Rachel. He thought that would get her attention and she would start to like him. Harley guessed that Arnold just didn't know much about girls. Harley tried to walk between her and the snowball throwers. He took several hits that were meant for her. When they got inside the school Rachel touched Harley's arm and told him thanks for keeping the snowballs from hitting her. When she said that, Harley felt no more pain from the hits he took from Arnold and his gang.

Things were going good. At ten o'clock Miss June's class started. This was what Harley had been waiting for. He wanted to know more about Rachel and he figured her short story would tell him some things that would help him impress her.

She started out by telling the title of her story. The title was 'The Friend I Loved'. It was all about this little dog that she was given when she was only four years old. His name was 'Muffin'. He was just a little ball of fur. It seemed he could even smile at you sometimes. When it came time for the little dog to go to his bed, he would come and scratch her on the foot. He was very smart. He only barked when strangers came to the door.

The story went on and on about the tricks that 'Muffin' would do. Rachel said in her story that she was never lonely when he was with her. Some of the girls in the class started to sniff a little. Rachel went on with her story about how little Muffin had been the joy of her life until he was taken from her by a gang of mean people riding bicycles. She had been visiting her cousin in Russellville before she moved to Mt. Hope. The little cousin had a broken leg and needed cheering up, so Rachel took Muffin with her. The tricks he could do would surely make cousin Annabelle laugh a lot. Sure enough, the tricks did the job. Annabelle was feeling great when Rachel left her house. Rachel was waiting for her dad in front of her cousin's house with Muffin. A band of thieves came riding by on bicycles and grabbed little Muffin. Away they peddled. They were out of sight when her dad arrived.

The sheriff was told about the thieves stealing little Muffin. He told Rachel's dad that he was on their trail and would let him know if he caught them. When Rachel finished reading her short story the whole class stood up and clapped and clapped for her. They liked her story even more than they had liked Harley's. Since it was her, he guessed it was o.k. for them to like her story more than his. He thought it was a little sad.

Now that he had heard her story, he had some new ideas about how to impress her. He would find 'Muffin' for her or he would find her one just like him. This would be his goal for the coming year.

When the class was over and recess began Harley headed for the principal's office. Not many boys ever wanted to be near that place, but Harley had some business there. When Mr. Childers saw Harley, he told him to come in and have a seat. The principal asked him how his family was? Harley replied that everyone was doing good. He then asked Mr. Childers if he knew if the school had ever burned? The answer that Mr. Childers gave was very interesting to Harley. "Yes, it burned, sometime back around 1930, I think. But why do you ask this question Harley?" This was going to be hard to explain to the principal. He finally answered that he may decide to do a research paper on Mt. Hope School sometime.

The other question that he had for Principal Childers was, did he know who paid to rebuild the school after it had burned? Mr. Childers said that he didn't know for sure, but he had heard that it was some rich man that had struck gold. Those answers were good enough for Harley. It just confirmed what he had dreamed was pretty near what had really happened. Harley thought, 'I probably will include some of this information in my long story in Miss June's class.'

When recess was over it was time to go back to homeroom and wait for the bell to go home. That is when all the announcements were made pertaining to the school and community. It was announced that Friday night of the next week there was going to be a box supper at the school gym. This was where all the girls in the school brought a box with food in it. The girl would stand on the stage with her box supper and the people in the audience would bid on the box of food. Also the girl had to eat the supper with the one that bid the most for it. This always caused a lot of excitement at the school.

Sometimes the most ugly boy had the most money and he would bid the highest on the prettiest girl's box of supper. She then had to eat with him. Harley almost immediately began to figure out where he could make some money. He knew right away the box that he was going to bid on. He just hoped he could sell enough eggs and scrap iron to the rolling store man to be able to bid the most on that box. He would be spending a lot of time with his metal detector for the next few days. He would welcome finding old horseshoes and old metal buckets. Mr. Howard would pay two cents a pound for good clean metal when his rolling store came around.

He thought he knew where there were at least two big hen nests. Maybe they would have twelve eggs each in them. He could get eighteen cents for a dozen eggs.

When boarding the bus for home that day, Harley was able to get a seat right behind Rachel. She always sat on the front row. As the bus rumbled on toward home, Harley finally got up the nerve to ask Rachel a question. He leaned forward and asked her, "Rachel, what will you put in your box?"

She replied, "I am not sure, but what do you like to eat?"

Harley was so shocked by her answer that he couldn't answer for a few minuets. She was saying to him that he had better get up the money to buy her box. He finally answered that banana sandwiches would be good.

He couldn't wait for the bus to pull to a stop in front of his house. He was off and in the house as quick as he could. Eating his cookie and drinking his glass of milk didn't take near as long as it usually did. He had other things more important to do. He grabbed his metal detector and out the door he went.

HARLEY AND THE BOX SUPPER

Harley had been trying to think where he might find the most scrap iron with his detector ever since the box supper was announced. He wished he had time to go to Soapstone Cave and dig for the treasure but that would just have to wait for a while. He would make a full-scale search of the cave when the weather warmed up. Springtime was just around the corner. Besides making money for the box supper, he also now had to begin to save for Valentine's Day. He sure hoped Mr. Jim-So got in his supply of valentine candy.

As Harley searched around the old machinery shed, he remembered something that happened last year when he and his daddy were cooking out lard from the hog meat. The big wash pot that they were using got so hot that it cracked when it began to cool off. It could no longer be used to cook out lard in. The pot must weigh at least fifty pounds. At two cents a pound, that thing would be worth a dollar when he sold it to the rolling store man. Mr. Howard also liked to buy old butter and grease. It was used to help make bombs for the war.

After he located the broken wash pot he was back to searching with the metal detector. Not far from the water well the buzzer went off. He got the shovel and dug about six inches into the ground. Something was wrapped in what looked like a piece of deerskin. Inside was an old civil war pistol. It was so rusty you could hardly tell what it was.

Harley remembered from his dreams that old Colonel Abel Straight had camped right across the road from where he lived during the war. He also remembered that the 500 soldiers were riding mules. There bound to be a lot of old metal horseshoes buried around his yard and garden. Mr. Howard would probably give him at least fifty cents for the old rusty pistol.

After searching with his metal detector for several days, after he got home from school, he had collected fourteen horseshoes, a part of an old metal plow, the army pistol, part of an old hoe, a broken tea kettle and the big broken wash pot. The rolling store man gave him a total of $2.25 for all of it.

Harley's daddy reminded him that the peanuts needed to be picked off when he was out of school Saturday. Each year his family had a patch of peanuts and old Tom and Ella were hitched up to the middle buster plow to rip them out of the ground. It was Harley's job to gather all the peanut vines up and shake the dirt off them and pile them up around a big post. Sometimes the pile of peanuts, which was called a shock of peanuts, was six feet tall and about as wide. When they were stored in such a way, the rains would wash all the dirt off them. Later in the winter Harley would take two empty buckets out to the shock of peanuts and sit on one bucket and fill the other with peanuts.

He figured that the box of supper he wanted to buy would cost him at least $5.00. When he went to the supper last year, he remembered that two boys had bid against each other for the homecoming queen's box. The winner had to pay $6.01 for it.

Harley really needed to make some more money before the big night. He told his daddy about his plans to bid on Rachel's box, since she was new in the school. He said that he didn't want her to feel overlooked since no one knew her. He asked his dad if he picked off three big buckets of peanuts Saturday could he sell one of them to Mr. Jim-So. He always bought some peanuts to resell at his store. Harley had never picked off more than one bucket of peanuts in a day before so his daddy thought he would go along with the deal.

Well, when the sun went down on Saturday, Harley was still picking off peanuts. He had two buckets picked off but after he had finished supper, he went back to the shock of peanuts. He was lucky that the moon was shinning so bright. His fingers were cold and stiff when he finally finished the third bucket of peanuts.

This was one Saturday night that he wished that he could go on to bed without getting in the wash tub, but he was too dirty to go to bed and so he washed all the peanut dirt off and jumped in the bed. He would sell his peanuts to Mr. Jim-So on Monday after school. Counting what he had saved in his snuff jar, he had $3.45. With the sale of the peanuts he would be getting close to the $5.00 he needed. As he drifted off to sleep he was thinking that there must be an easier way to impress a girl than buying her box of supper.

Harley could barely turn the pages in his bible during Sunday school the next morning. His fingers were stiff as a board. It was hard for the Sunday school teacher to get everyone quiet that morning. They all wanted to talk about the box supper. He overheard Arnold tell Billy Hugh that he was going to bid high on Rachel's box.

When he heard Arnold say that he wished that Uncle Avis and Aunt Minnie had never moved up here from Newburg. Arnold was always causing trouble.

All during Sunday school and preaching, Harley could barely keep his mind from thinking about the box supper. He really needed some scripture to give him some assurance about the big night. He finally decided that God was not in the box supper business.

By the end of the service he decided that the money from the sale of the boxes would go for a good cause and he was justified in his desire to be the winner of the bidding for Rachel's box. He also decided that he needed a little more money to be sure he had enough to win the bid for the box.

There had been several boys that had really liked the cowboy boots that his cousin, Danny, had sent him. They were getting a little tight on his feet so he thought he would put out the word that he would take $2.00 for them. By the time school was out on Monday there had been three boys that wanted to buy them. One of them was Arnold. This would be good. Arnold would spend some of his box supper money on the boots and that would give him a better chance to outbid him. He told Arnold to bring his money the next day and he could have the boots.

When Harley got home from school he, as usual, grabbed his cookie and glass of milk. After finishing his refreshments it was off to Mr. Jim-So's store with the peanuts. Mr. Jim-So was glad to see Harley and his peanuts. He weighed them out and told Harley that he had fifteen pounds and that he would give him ten cents per pound. That would amount to $1.50. That would bring his total available funds so far to $4.95. With the $2.00 from the boots he would have $6.95.

That would be an awful lot to pay for a couple of banana sandwiches, but it would be worth it to get to buy Rachel's box. He would get to sit by her while they ate.

The big night finally came. It was the largest crowd of the year at the school, except for graduation night. The banker, the cotton ginner, the four storeowners, and the preacher were there. All the teachers were there also. The lady teachers all brought their supper boxes. Every boy in school was there along with some who had graduated the year before. Harley became really nervous. He couldn't wait for the bidding to start.

The cotton ginner's daughter was the first to have her box auctioned off. Some real ugly boy started to bid on her box. She almost cried when she saw him bidding, but her daddy came to her rescue. He won the bid with $3.75.

The next girl was the homecoming queen. All the big basketball stars bid on her box. They must have not scrapped much cotton, because they would only raise the bid five cents each time. Her box brought $3.05. The basketball manager won the bid. Next was Miss June's box.

There were three bachelors in the town and all of them were struck on Miss June. They started bidding. They all had good jobs and probably were making $20.00 a week. A red headed man was the high bidder. His name was Ted and he had to bid $7.55 to get Miss June's box. About thirty more boxes were sold before Rachel's box was auctioned off.

Harley was watching Arnold real close to see if he was going to bid. The bidding started. Her daddy, the preacher, was the first to bid. He bid $2.00. Then the banker raised him by bidding $3.00. Harley got more nervous. He knew he could not out bid the banker. Then he saw Arnold hold up his hand and he bid $3.01. Rachel laughed. Harley knew then that Arnold must have spent all his money on his used cowboy boots. It was now time for him to get into the bidding. Harley bid $3.50. The preacher bid $3.75. The banker bid $4.00. Harley thought he may as well go ahead and show them that he was in the game to stay so he bid $5.00.

The crowd clapped for him. The banker didn't know what to think about the crowd cheering Harley, so he figured that he would stop his bidding. He did not want to lose any business at the bank. Harley won the bid and got to eat with Rachel.

He said later to Arnold that those were the best banana sandwiches he had ever eaten.

HARLEY PLANTS TOMATO PLANTS

Harley, decided that having a girl friend just took too much time and effort. He could buy enough bananas for the $5.00 he had spent at the box supper to make at least a 100 banana sandwiches. He was just glad that he didn't have to spend all the money he had made for Rachel's box supper. He could buy a lot of batteries for the detector and flashlight that he would be needing later. He couldn't wait for warmer weather to go back to the mountain.

Valentine's day came and went. Harley decided that he wouldn't even ask Mr. Jim-So about the valentine candy. He did make himself buy a ten cent card for Rachel. She would get so many valentine cards that he figured his would not even be read. He had learned his lesson about spending a lot of money on girls. Arnold was smarter than he had given him credit for. At least he had spent his box supper money on a good pair of Texas boots. Down deep he wished he still had the boots, even though they were a little tight on his feet. He had heard that sometimes boys did dumb things when it came to girls. The rest of the weeks of winter passed slowly for Harley. He had so much planned for springtime, he would have no time for girls.

When Saturday, April 15th finally did arrive it was time for one of Harley's favorite days. Actually, he had started planning for this day back on Thanksgiving Day of last year. That was the day that he always planted his tomato seed. He would make a little house about two feet long and one foot wide out of willow wood. He would make it so he could stretch some clear cellophane over the top of it. After placing some good barnyard soil in it he would place his better boy tomato seed in neat little rows and cover them with some clean sand. There was a window in the quilting room that would let just the right amount of sunlight to shine on the little greenhouse. The seed would sprout in about two or three weeks. Then the plants would be ready to set in the ground as the weather warmed. His daddy would always tell him and others to never plant tomatoes in the ground before April 15th.

Usually the danger of frost is past by mid April and the danger of the plants getting killed would be less. The plants would be taken to the garden and planted in the good earth where more barnyard soil had been added. They were then covered with a gallon glass jug for about ten days. The plants would then get used to being outside. Harley took great pride in picking the first ripe tomatoes in the community. Most years he would pick a ripe tomato by July 4th. Sometimes he even sold some of them to the rolling store and to Mr. Jim-So. Harley began to think more about making a few dollars than about girls. He also looked forward to Sundays. If he had sold anything during the week he always gave Jesus his share of it. His Sunday school teacher and his daddy quoted and read Malachi 3:10 to him many times. It said to give a tithe to God and the giver would be blessed many times over.

After working in the garden most of the day, Harley decided that it was good to work in the soil that God had made. He could work and think about a lot of things at the same time. Also while he was digging holes for the plants and bean seeds he would find some good long and fat fishing worms. They liked the good garden soil like his tomato plants did. He carried a can with him all the time when he was digging. They would come in handy when he went perch fishing down at the creek. Next week was the week of A.E.A. Harley would have a whole week to fish, and hunt treasure with his metal detector and to go to Soapstone Cave.

Sunday, when Rachel came into Sunday school class, Harley could hardly believe what he saw!!! Rachel had on lipstick!!! That was the last straw. He just looked at her and mumbled hello. He just about had girls off his mind and more important things to think about, like mountain climbing, treasure hunting, and fishing. Now she starts using lipstick. He sat as far away from her as he could. He even hoped Arnold would sit by her. He didn't need girls to occupy his mind, certainly not during A.E.A. Week. As Rachel's daddy, the preacher, was preaching, Harley wondered what he thought about his daughter wearing lipstick. Surely he hadn't noticed that she had it on.

After preaching and the ride home, Harley was ready to do some exploring. His daddy reminded him that his mama had fried chicken before church and that the hot biscuits and gravy would be ready in a few minutes. While he was waiting he got his bicycle out and tied his metal detector to it. The new water canteen would come in handy today since it had warmed up so much. He had won it in F.F.A. selling cans of peanuts. His agriculture teacher was always coming up with ideas about raising money to buy new shop tools.

Harley knew he wouldn't have time to climb all the way up to Soapstone Cave that evening, so he just decided to ride down to Mr. Jim-So's store. He always opened the store on Sunday evenings. When he got down to the store there were three or four men and some boys there, sitting on nail kegs. They were whittling on some pieces of cedar wood. They asked him what that thing he had on his bicycle was and he told them it was a metal detector. He said that a person could find buried money, horseshoes, or anything made of metal. They laughed and said that they had never heard of such a thing. One man said that he would give him a dime if he could find any money around the store.

Harley asked Mr. Jim-So if it would be all right for him to use the detector outside around the store. He said that it would be okay if he would give him half of what he found. Harley thought that was a pretty good deal, since it was on Mr. Jim-So's land The men followed Harley outside to get the detector and watch him use it. Just as quick as he turned the buzzer on, it started making a loud noise. Harley asked Mr. Jim-So if he had a shovel. Soon there were holes all over the dirt parking lot. The men couldn't believe what they had seen. Harley found pennies, dimes, quarters and bottle caps. All in all, Harley had uncovered ninety-eight cents. Mr. Jim-So got forty-nine cents and Harley got forty-nine cents. The man that offered the dime paid him also. Fifty-nine cents was not bad for a couple hours of treasure hunting. He told Mr. Jim-So that he would just buy that much in batteries.

After he peddled back home and done the things, he watered his newly planted tomatoes and gathered the eggs. There were two more hens setting on their eggs and would probably hatch out some new chicks next week. Harley liked the farm life almost as much as he liked treasure hunting. He wanted Monday morning to come quick and the best way for that to happen was for him to go to bed early and get up early.

It had been a busy week for Harley. The teachers were really bearing down on the students and there had been a lot of homework. The garden had been plowed and planted. Also, getting dressed up for church and with the shock of seeing Rachel wearing lipstick, had really made for a tiring week. So, sleep came quickly Sunday night. Before long he was dreaming. This time the dream was different from the ones he had been having. It was not about the hidden treasure, or Soapstone Cave.

HARLEY, THE DEPUTY

Harley's dream were somewhat unpredictable and tonight's dream was no exception. Maybe it was because his week had been so eventful in so many different ways. The visit to Mr. Jim-So's store had been a lot of fun. Mr. Franklin's chief deputy was in the group of men at the store. The other men called him Chief Dalton. Harley had heard of him and how brave he was. Not too long ago Harley had told Arnold that he wished he could be a deputy when he got big. He said if he could be one that the first thing he would do would be to arrest the Dufus McGee Gang. Another reason for his strange dream might have been that he was excited about being out of school for the whole week for A.E.A. There was so much for him to do, he would not know what to do first.

His Sunday night dream started out with a visit to the sheriff's office. He asked Chief Dalton where Mr. Franklin, the sheriff, was? The chief said he was gone to Montgomery to take some dangerous prisoners to the penitentiary. Two of the prisoners had been caught up in the Eckerberger Mountains making whiskey. When Mr. Franklin took an ax and cut up their whiskey still, that was hid in the woods, they ran, shooting their rifle and pistols at him. He just let them shoot until they ran out of bullets and then just walked over to where they were and told them, "It's time to go boys." Chief Dalton said they didn't put up much of a fuss when they saw the sheriff's long barreled pistol. He said that there were not too many moonshiners left since

Mr. Franklin got to be the sheriff. He had rather cut up a whiskey still than to eat when he was hungry.

Harley opened the jail door and Chief Dalton asked if he could help him. Harley replied that he guessed he could. He told the chief that he wanted to be a deputy sheriff. Well, the chief just about busted a gut laughing. He told Harley that if he would come back in about ten years that maybe they could use him as a deputy. That was not the answer Harley wanted to hear. He suggested to the chief that maybe he could be just a junior deputy. Chief Dalton thought that seemed to be a good solution to the problem. Dalton fumbled around the desk drawer and found an old badge and put it on Harley and said, "I, Chief Dalton, do hereby deputize you to be a junior deputy in Lawrence County, Alabama."

He then asked Harley why he wanted to be a deputy? The young junior deputy said that there were a bunch of bicycle thieves, called "The Dufus McGee Gang" and that they needed to be caught and sent to the pen. He said that they had been stealing bicycles since his daddy was a little boy. He added they were also wanted for stealing people's dogs.

It was too bad that the chief didn't give him a pistol to be deputy with. He would just have to use his cap pistol. It would shoot pretty loud and looked just like a real pistol. As Harley was on his way back towards home, he decided to do a little investigating. When he stopped at Mr. Jim-So's store, he asked him if he had seen any strange men riding bicycles around lately. Mr. Jim-So said, "Yes I have, they were here at the store just a few hours ago." He told Harley that they were a mean looking bunch of hombres. Harley became excited when he heard this. Which way did they go he asked? Mr. Jim-So said that they had started up the road toward the mountain.

Harley said, "Do you mean the Eckerberger Mountain?"

"Yep, that's the right mountain," Mr. Jim-So said.

"One more thing, Mr. Jim-So, did they have a dog with them?"

"They shore did, Harley, and you know what? I traded them out of him. I gave them all a big orange drink and a moon pie for him. He is right over there by the candy counter in a big paste board box." Sure enough the little dog was Muffin. He couldn't believe it.

Now what was he going to do about the gang? Should he go after them now or should he try to buy Muffin from Mr. Jim-So? He knew one thing. There was a certain girl that would sure like to have her dog back.

About that time he heard a car come sliding up to the gas pumps. Sheriff Franklin got out of the patrol car and came into the store. He said, "Hi there Deputy Harley Earle. How many crooks have you caught today?" Deputy Harley couldn't wait to tell him about the Dufus McGee Gang. The sheriff said he had been on their trail for a long time and he would go up in the mountains tomorrow and catch them. They needed to be put in jail. They had caused too many kids to go to bed at night, crying, because someone had stolen their bicycles. Harley was glad to hear the sheriff was going to get the crooks.

As Harley dreamed on, he told Mr. Jim-So that if he had any trouble to just let him know and he would be down to the store as quick as he could. Just remember that his telephone number was three longs and one short. Before he left the store he asked how much he would take for little Muffin. Mr. Jim-So told him that he guessed the little dog was worth about $2.00. The young deputy said that he would probably be back in a day or two and buy the dog. Harley Earle decided that girls were expensive, even in dreams.

Harley awoke early the next morning. He was a little confused. He had thought that the Dufus McGee Gang had left for Arkansas. The dream was so real that he thought that they must be in the area again. He continued to think about the gang. And there was something else that kept bugging him. Was little Muffin really down at Mr. Jim-So's store?

Harley's mom told him that breakfast was ready and he had better eat a lot if he planned to go hiking. He ate in a hurry that morning and was outside in a flash to do the things. When he brought the milk into the house he asked his mom where his daddy was and she said that he was out by the garden. He had heard noises during the night and he thought it might be that old armadillo that had been eating up the sweet potatoes. They were buried in the soil and straw outside by the car shed. Harley went out to see about his tomatoes. His dad said that everything was all right and that it must have been something else that was making the noise.

When he went back to the house, he began to fill his knapsack with biscuits and ham and his canteen with water. He was ready to get on his way to Soapstone Cave. He told his mama good-bye and was out the door with his metal detector to get on his bicycle.

The only thing was, the bicycle was nowhere to be found. It didn't take Harley long to figure out what had happened. He was so sound asleep that he didn't fully wake up last night when the Dufus McGee Gang had stolen his bicycle. He heard the thieves just enough to make him dream about them. This called for some real action.

He decided to tell his daddy the whole story. After hearing what Harley had to say, his daddy knew that it was time to call in Sheriff Franklin. He got on the phone to the operator and told her to connect him to the sheriff's office. Chief Deputy Dalton said that he had been gone since daylight. He was up in the Eckerberger Mountain looking for some thieves.

HARLEY HELPS CAPTURE THE BICYCLE THIEVES

This new development was no dream. Harley's bicycle was really stolen and the Dufus McGee Gang were really alive and here in Mt. Hope. It was most surely a fact that they had swapped little Muffin to Mr. Jim-So for some orange drinks and moon pies. He didn't know this for sure, but he would go to the store as quick as he could and see if Muffin was there. He had heard that sometimes dreams do come true. He hoped that the dream he had last night did. He guessed he could spare a little time to take Muffin to Rachel if he could get up the $2.00 Mr. Jim-So wanted for him.

When Harley's daddy said that the sheriff was going up into the Eckerberger Mountains to look for the thieves, Harley got a little nervous. He wanted his bicycle back but he was afraid that someone would find Soapstone Cave before he had a chance to dig up any treasure that was in it. He told his daddy that he wanted to go with him if he went up into the mountain. His daddy thought about it and finally agreed to let him go with him. They rode the truck as far as they could go up the mountain. When they got out, Harley told his daddy to be sure and get the keys out of the truck because the thieve were probably looking at them through their spyglass. He knew they had one, because he had seen it hanging on one of the gang's bicycles earlier.

Maybe they didn't get up early enough to see the sheriff when he started up the mountain. He reasoned that the gang probably slept late this morning because they were up so late last night stealing his bicycle. They soon caught up with Mr. Franklin. The sheriff was not too happy to get their help. He thought that the gang most likely had guns, but Harley told him that he had run into the gang before and that as far as he could tell they did not carry any guns. He also knew that they always stole stuff when there was no one around and that they knew from past experience in Arkansas that if they were caught with a gun that their jail sentence would be longer.

As the three made their way on up the mountain they came to a fork in the path. Harley knew where they were hiding the time that they had warned him about being in their mountain. He told the sheriff that he knew the mountain pretty well and that he had seen the gang go up the path to the left. Another reason he told the sheriff to take the path to the left was that the path to the right was the path that would take them to Soapstone Cave. He didn't want anyone else to know about the cave, even the sheriff.

Sure enough, about a mile further on up the path, they began to see a little curl of smoke. The thieves were up and cooking their breakfast. As they peeped through the trees and brush they could see that they had a skillet on their campfire. Harley was sure he heard one of the crooks telling the others that that old setting hen sure hated to give up her eggs last night. Not only had they stolen Harley's bicycle, but had went to the hen house and stole the old setting hen's eggs. They were meaner than Harley had thought. He guessed the old hen was lucky she wasn't in the frying pan.

Mr. Franklin told them to stay where they were and he would work his way to the other side and when he came out of the brush with his big pistol for them to holler loud that they were surrounded. He figured that they would think they were surrounded by a whole posse of deputies. Sheriff

Franklin came out of the brush with his pistol firing into the air. Harley and his daddy came out hollering that they were surrounded and to put their hands in the air. The bicycle thieves were so surprised and scared that they all did what they were told to do except their leader, Dufus McGee. He ran into the brush and trees. He didn't even have on his boots. The sheriff said to let him go that they would get him later. He handcuffed the other four thieves and began to ask them questions. He learned that they had indeed been the ones to steal Harley's bicycle and the setting hen's eggs.

The eggs were burned to a crisp by this time. The crooks would just have to go hungry until they got to the Lawrence County jail. There were ten bicycles hid over in the brush. The sheriff made the four push and carry down the mountain two bicycles each. Harley's daddy pushed one and he pushed his own.

Mr. Franklin walked behind the prisoners and told them that they had better not try anything foolish. When they got to the bottom of the mountain, all the bicycles, except Harley's, were placed in their truck. The sheriff had asked Harley's daddy if he would bring them in to his office. He knew some little kids would be glad to come in and claim theirs.

Harley was worried about Dufus McGee. Would he be in the mountains waiting for him when he went back to Soapstone Cave? He knew that Dufus couldn't get too far without his boots. The sheriff had brought his boots down with him to his car. He said that he would be back tomorrow with a dog to track him down. It would be easy for the dog to track him because his bare feet would leave a clear scent for him to follow. Harley decided to wait a day or two before going back into the mountain to give the sheriff time to catch the crook.

Harley and his daddy were back home in time to eat dinner. Since it was A.E.A. week, Harley's daddy had taken a weeks vacation from his work at the oil company and had planned to do some work around the farm. The tractor needed tuning up and the plows needed repairing. Harley looked forward to helping him.

Harley figured that he had better find a few more eggs to sell Mr. Jim-So. He had $1.95 and only needed another nickel to have the $2.00 for little Muffin. Mr. Jim-So was giving two cents per egg now. Finding six eggs was no trouble at all. He would have enough money for Muffin and some left over for some juicy fruit chewing gum. That was the kind that Rachel liked. In spite of his desire to forget about girls, he still wanted to do things that he thought would please Rachel.

He became more nervous as he peddled closer to the store. Was the dream really going to come true? Would little Muffin really be there? Would Mr. Jim-So really sell the dog to him for $2.00? As he entered the store the first thing he noticed was that there was no box where he had dreamed it was the night before. There was no little dog anywhere inside the store that he could see. Mr. Jim-So asked him what he could do for him. Harley put the little sack of eggs on the counter and said he would like to sell his eggs and get a pack of juicy fruit. Mr. Jim-So gave him the juicy fruit gum and 7 cents back in change. Harley now had $2.02.

Mr. Jim-So asked Harley had he seen the sheriff this morning. He told Mr. Jim-So about the trip up in the mountains and about catching four of the bicycle thieves that had been going around stealing stuff. And that sometimes they even stole little dogs. Mr. Jim-So began to really listen close when he mentioned about stealing dogs. He told Harley that he had seen the thieves just yesterday and they left a little dog with him. They said that they didn't have anything to feed it and it was hungry. Harley knew then that some dreams do come almost true. He told Mr. Jim-So that his preacher's girl had lost a little dog and would like to have one. He finally got up the courage to ask Mr. Jim-So how much he would take for the little dog. Mr. Jim-So thought about it a little while and finally said that since it was the preacher's girl wanting a dog that he guessed he would just give it to her. Boy, was that good news for Harley.

Harley thought about the situation for a while and finally told Mr. Jim-So that he would tell the preacher about the dog. He also told him to be on the lookout for Dufus McGee, that he was still on the loose and he might come to the store looking to buy or steal some shoes or boots since the sheriff had taken his to the jail after the raid on the crooks camp. Mr. Jim-So thanked Harley for the warning.

It was only about a mile on down the road to where the preacher lived. Harley peddled toward the house slowly. When he got close he saw Rachel on the front porch. She saw him. He couldn't turn back now. He peddled right up to where she was swinging. He could think of no other way to say what he came to tell her so he just blurted out that he had found her dog. She told Harley that he should not be telling fibs and that she thought he was a better boy than that and that it made her sad to even to think about her little Muffin. Harley didn't have much experience in dealing with girls, especially if they looked like they were going to burst out crying. About that time, the preacher came out on the porch and asked what was going on. Harley related the story about the thieves and about Mr. Jim-So having the little dog. The preacher was more trusting of Harley and said they would drive up to the store to check out his story.

Harley peddled after the preacher's car and arrived at the store in time to see Rachel pick up and hug little

Muffin. He decided he would just keep on peddling toward home. Girls were sure strange creatures.

Well at least part of the dream came true. He figured that someday he may even still become a deputy sheriff.

HARLEY OVERSLEEPS

The A.E.A. holidays would come to a close before long. He had to get on with the plan that he had, concerning locating the treasure in Soapstone Cave. He knew it was bound to be there, it was just a matter of finding the time to locate it. After such a long day with the sheriff and the bicycle thieves, not to mention reuniting little Muffin with his rightful owner, Harley was just worn out. He decided he best get in bed early and get a good night's sleep. As soon as he finished his chores and ate his supper, he was ready to hit the bed.

In just a few minuets he was fast asleep. When Harley was real tired, he always dreamed a lot. This night was no different. He dreamed and dreamed and dreamed. The only thing was that all the dreams were different from other dreams he had been having. They were much shorter. Sort of like short stories. Harley Earle's first dreamed concerned being a dog and cat doctor. It went something like this.

Dr. Harley Earle got a call from one of the men in the community of Newburg. He was known as one of the richest men in all of Franklin County. He told Harley that if he could come down and doctor one of his wife's cats that had come to their house that he would be well rewarded. It seemed that someone had tied a tin can to its' little tail and turned it loose to run wild. Harley thought for a moment and in the back of his mind something bothered him. He couldn't quite put his finger on it, but he had heard of some mean boys doing something like that before. He got his

153

medicine bag and saddled up Flicka, his horse, and headed out to Mr. Jewel's house.

When he got to Mr. Jewel's house, his wife was holding the little cat in her arms. Dr. Harley looked at the little cat and tears began to come to his eyes. He remembered now what and when this had happened. He became very ashamed. He took the little cat and applied some of the medicine from his doctor's bag to it's injured tail.

After a little while, the little kitten was purring and seemed to be feeling better. When Mr. Jewel tried to pay Dr. Harley, he would take no money for his services and told him if the kitten didn't get well soon to call him again. He told Deanie, Mr. Jewel's wife, that he would put out the word that if anybody was caught doing this to a cat again that they would be turned in to Sheriff Franklin and he would take care of them.

Harley became very restless and woke up. The dream had been a good one for Harley to have. If Arnold or anyone else ever wanted to tie a tin can to a cat again they would have him to deal with. Or better still, they would have Sheriff Franklin to deal with. He also figured that there would be better ways to clean out the stovepipes in their kitchen. He also decided that not only do dreams sometimes come true, but they also teach lessons to people, especially to boys.

As Harley drifted off to sleep again, probably just the thought about Mr. Franklin dealing with cat criminals made him dream about being a deputy again. Anyway, Harley dreamed that he was back at the sheriff's office to get his next assignment.

Chief Deputy Dalton told him about this crook that was breaking into people's houses and stealing shoes and boots. It was as if the crook was looking for a certain kind of boot. Most of the time they would be found outside the house. Deputy Dalton figured the crook must be trying them on and if they didn't fit then he would leave them and go on to the next house.

Junior Deputy Harley Earle knew right away who that crook was. He was the same man that had left his boots when Mr. Franklin had captured most of the bicycle gang. Then he told Deputy Dalton that he could put out the word to look for Dufus McGee that he had good information that Dufus was defiantly in the market for some new footwear.

After leaving the sheriff's office Harley put in a call to his uncle's house and asked to speak to Arnold. He was going to warn him about the boot crook. Arnold came to the phone but could hardly talk for snubbing. Harley asked him what was the matter and Arnold blurted out that someone had broke into their house last night and stole his Texas boots. This time the boots were not left on the porch. The boot crook had worn them as he went down the road toward Russellville. Harley really hated to hear this because he thought that at some time in the future that he would be able to talk Arnold into selling them back to him.

Harley woke himself up when he bumped his head on the bedpost. He was on the floor looking for his boots. When he found them he put them in the bed with him. If Dufus got his boots, he would have to get him too. These dreams were making Harley tired. He wished it was time to get up but it was only midnight. It took a while for Harley to get back to sleep and he had a lot of time to think about what he was going to do the next day. There just had to be a way for him to get to Soapstone Cave before the A.E.A. holidays were over.

As the hours passed, Harley finally went back to sleep, but not before he had worked out his plan for his trip to the mountain the next day. His plan was for him to get up early and do the things, eat a big breakfast and help his daddy fix the broken middle buster plow. He would fill his canteen with water and fix a lot of peanut butter sandwiches, get a few cookies and put it all in his knapsack. He would check the batteries in his metal detector and flashlight and put air in his bicycle tires. He would then be ready for the big day at Soapstone Cave. He could hardly wait until tomorrow. Then he began to drift back into a deep sleep.

Harley's mama and daddy were eating a late breakfast. Just the two of them. They were talking to each other about hearing Harley talking to himself in his sleep last night. He had been mumbling something about his boots. Then they heard a big thump. It had been Harley falling out of his bed. He sometimes had dreams and walked in his sleep, so they didn't think anything about it. He always got back in his bed after he awoke from his dream. Harley's daddy said that ever now and then a young boy deserved to sleep late and since this was his school vacation week that it would be all right for him to stay in bed until dinner time.

Needless to say, Harley was very disappointed about not making the climb to the mountain cave that day but promised himself that tomorrow would be the day he had been waiting for. He would surely go to the cave the next day. By sundown the next day, he would have some of that treasure in his hands.

Harley Opens the Chest

HARLEY OPENS THE CHEST

Sleeping late always made Harley sort of drowsy the rest of the new day. When he finally did get up and move around a little, he got to feeling better. His day was spent mostly thinking about what he was determined to do the next day. He prepared as much as he could for the long climb up Eckerberger Mountain. He would need good luck to have time to the reach the cave and dig for the treasure and then get back home before dark. He still was a little afraid to be on the mountain after dark with Dufus McGee still on the loose. Dufus was a little man but Harley was sure that the outlaw knew some bad tricks that he could pull on him.

The metal detector had not been used lately, so he thought he best try it out a little before he made the climb the next day. Just about every time he used the metal detector around his house and yard, he would find old rifle balls. They had probably been shot when Col. Abel Straight and his men camped across the fence from his house. They had made their headquarters right across the road in the old Templeton plantation house. Harley wondered sometimes just how big Mt. Hope would be now if Col. Straight and his men had passed on through the area instead of tearing everything up so bad. He guessed they were just trying to find all the money in the town. It is said that the town of Mt. Hope was really a growing town before the war.

The buzzer started to sound off as he neared the fence between his daddy's and Mr. Boty's land. There was an old tree on the fence line and it was just about rotted down. The buzzer was getting louder. The closer to the old tree, the louder it sounded. Harley kicked at the stump of the old cedar tree. Part of the dead wood fell away and sure enough there was something inside the dead tree. Well it was not a bucket full of money, but it was an old tin box. It must have been there about ninety years. That would have been about when history books said that the Union Army camped over night in Mt. Hope. They were on their way to fight General Forrest. Anyway, inside the tin box were some silver dollars. The discovery was enough to convince Harley that the metal detector was in good working shape. He did decide to ride down to Mr. Jim-So's store and get a pair of new batteries just in case he needed them for the detector or the flashlight.

When Harley Earle rode up to the store, he saw that the preacher and Rachel was just pulling away. They waved to Harley. When he went inside the store, Mr. Jim-So started laughing. He told Harley that the preacher's girl was asking about him. Harley just listened. Finally Mr. Jim-So said she was glad that you told her about little Muffin being up here at my store. He went on to tell Harley that he thought she was a little bit struck on him. Harley still just listened. There was more important things on his mind than girls right now. After visiting with Shelby and Sherman, who had stopped by to get gas, Harley asked Mr. Jim-So how many batteries could he get for nineteen cents? The storeowner allowed he would let him have two batteries, but that they would normally be twenty cents for the two.

As he peddled back home, he couldn't help but smile when he thought about what Rachel said to Mr. Jim-So. He decided that maybe if things went good, he may just ask her to go to the picture show when he was about twenty years old. Right now he just had too much on his mind to think about girls. When Harley got home it was time to do the things. After supper and after he listened to gangbusters on the radio, he hit the hay.

When morning came the bright light woke him up. The light had not been turned on but the room was as light as if it was in the middle of the day. Harley was very upset that he had overslept again. He jumped up and put his clothes on and looked out the window. Was he ever so surprised? The ground was as white as snow. If fact it was snow.

During the night it had come a surprise snowstorm. It had never snowed in April as long as he had been alive. Why, oh why, did it have to snow this time? He had such big plans for the day. He began to think, what will I do now about the climb to Soapstone Cave? He also thought he had better check on his tomato plants and see if the glass jars had protected them from the cold. He was relieved to see that they were all right. He hurried on back to the house for breakfast which was about ready. Big snows and big breakfasts always went together. The scrambled eggs, country ham and red eye gravy took Harley's mind off of Soapstone Cave while he ate. After eating he was wide awake and his mind was in high gear. He finally figured out how he was going to get to Soapstone Cave.

Harley asked his daddy if he could hitch old Ella up to the sled and go for a ride. His daddy said that he did that when he was a boy and he guessed it would be alright for him to do the same thing.

When he hitched old Ella up to the sled he piled on twelve ears of corn. He didn't want the horse to get hungry while he waited on him to make his climb. He was careful to put every thing on the sled that he needed. He was sure to take a couple of extra empty sacks to put the treasure in. He was sure he was going to find a lot of things that the Jessie James Gang had buried in the cave.

Soon, Harley was on his way. Riding the sled on snow was almost as much fun as looking for buried treasure. Old

Ella seemed to enjoy the snow also. She would trot for a little while and stop to sniff the snow. Sometimes she licked it. She would be all right while Harley made the climb. He knew just the place to leave the sled and old Ella. There was a flat place with some tall rocks beside it. The wind and cold would not be bad there at all. When they got to the spot, Harley unhitched Ella from the sled and tied her up to a tree. The rope was plenty long enough for her to walk around a little and lick on some snow. He placed her corn where she could get it without any trouble and began to gather up his gear for the climb.

It was pretty slick in some places and by the time he got up to the cave, he was about give out. A little snow and some peanut butter and crackers gave him new energy. Energy to dig. He began to look around for the spot he was digging in when he had to leave the last time he was in the cave. Finally, he located it. This time he had brought a little short handled shovel to dig with. It was small but plenty strong enough to do what he needed to do. He raked the limbs and leaves away from the spot and started to dig.

About that time he heard some loud noises. The noise sounded like some airplanes flying. Soon he felt the air moving over his head. Harley began to think that there were ghost all around him. He reached for his flashlight and turned it on and pointed it toward the top of the cave. He was relieved to see that there were hundreds of bats flying out of the cave. They were soon all gone. When his heart settled down, he started back to digging. He struck something hard. It was the metal chest that he had found before.

There was a lot of digging to do before he was able to drag it out of the hole. As he expected, it had an old rusty lock on it. This time he was ready for anything. He had brought a hammer and chisel with him. He began to hit the lock. It was still in good shape and hard to break. But it did.

Harley was out of breath. He didn't know whether to raise the top to the chest or not. He just sat for a moment and looked at it. He finally got up the courage to raise the top. It had been such a long time since he first began his search for the treasure. Anyway the time had finally come. As he slowly lifted the top, dust arose from inside the trunk.

Harley Becomes the Hero

HARLEY BECOMES A HERO

Harley's heart was beating very hard. He removed a piece of deer hide that was spread over what ever was in the box. When he lifted the hide he saw it. The treasure that he had been dreaming of was right in front of his eyes.

There were stacks of $20 bills. Each bundle of bills had a wrapper around them. He could barely read what was on the wrapper. The printing was almost faded out but the best he could tell it said 'Wells Fargo'. That must have been the bank that the James Gang had taken the money from. Harley laid the deer skin out on the floor of the cave and then put the stacks of money on it. There were fifty bundles of money in the chest. Each bundle had fifty of the $20 dollar bills in it. Harley figured in his head that the chest must have about a total of $50,000 in it. What in the world would he do with that much money?

Again, Harley asked himself, 'what am I going to do with all that money'? He just then began to realize that to be that rich was going to be a lot of trouble. He didn't know whether to turn on his metal detector and look for more treasure now that he was already rich or just go on back down the mountain to old Ella and go home. After thinking about the situation for a while he decided that the best thing to do right then was to get the money in his knapsack and head on back towards home. He knew it was going to take a lot of talking and explaining to his daddy what he had been up to the last few months. Harley had been very secretive about his Soapstone Cave adventures.

The snow had melted some and froze again. The path down the mountain was very slippery. As Harley made his way down to old Ella, he kept thinking about the words, 'Wells Fargo'. He had heard of a bank of that name somewhere.

Ella was a very faithful friend. She was still tied to the tree and seemed glad to see Harley again. While he was untying her he noticed a piece of paper hanging on to a limb. He got the paper and read the following note. 'I know what you were doing on my mountain. I want the money. Leave it in the hollow tree beside your house. I will get it before daylight tomorrow.' The note was not signed, but Harley knew who it was. There had been only one person that had claimed Eckerberger Mountain as his own. That would be Dufus McGee. Harley also saw his boot prints in the snow. They were the prints of his Texas boots.

Harley wasted little time in hitching up Ella to the sled and headed for home. As soon as he got home and put old Ella in the barn, he headed to the house to find his daddy. He was sure glad he had taken the week off from the Standard Oil Company in Russellville and was home today.

Sounds were coming from the tractor shed. His daddy was just finishing repairing the middle buster plow. That was good. Harley said, "Daddy, I have something very important to talk to you about." They sat down by the stove in the shed and Harley began to tell his daddy the whole story about Soapstone Cave and the buried treasure. He even told him about the dreams he had about the Jessie James Gang. Then he got his knapsack and poured the money out on the floor. Harley's daddy almost fainted when he saw all that money. Harley said he guessed it was about $50,000 dollars. He then pointed out the bands around the bundles of money. "This was probably stolen from the Wells Fargo bank," Harley said. The printing on the bands could still be read. Harley's daddy asked him what he thought they should do with the money. His daddy was hoping Harley would give him the right answer. After a few moments, Harley responded that the money was most likely stolen from the Wells Fargo bank and it should be returned to them.

There was just one more thing that he needed to share with his daddy. He needed to tell him about Dufus McGee. He showed the note to his daddy. Harley was really glad that his daddy knew the whole story now, because he knew just what to do about the crook. They gathered up the money and went to the house and put in a call to Sheriff Franklin. The good sheriff said that he would park his car down at Mr. Jim-So's store and walk to their house after dark. He would wait close to the hollow tree until Dufus showed up. The rest would be easy when old Dufus reached inside the hollow tree to get the money the sheriff would slip up behind and arrest him. If he ran, he would lose the race because the sheriff never lost a foot race.

The plan was a good one. Now all they had to do was wait on the thief to show up. Sleep was not an option as far as Harley was concerned, he was going to stay awake until Dufus was caught by the sheriff. His daddy said that they would turn out all the lights and pretend to be asleep. He knew Dufus would not make a move to get the money until all was quiet around their house. As soon as supper was finished and an empty sack was put in the hollow tree, the lights were turned off. The family sat around the stove. Even though it was the middle of April, the late snow made for a cold night.

The long climb up Eckerberger Mountain carrying all the digging equipment and metal detector had caused Harley to be about worn out. It was all he could do to stay awake. He was just about to doze off around midnight when he heard the sheriff holler, "Put your hands up or I will shoot." Then there was silence. It seemed forever before another sound was heard.

Finally, he heard Sheriff Franklin call for his daddy to come out and see what he had caught.

The old bicycle thief looked like he may have had a rough winter. He was walking like his feet were hurting him. Harley found out later that the boots that he had stolen from Arnold's house were too small for his big feet. Dufus liked them so much that he wore them just the same. Anyway, the sheriff handcuffed him and walked him all the way to Mr. Jim-So's store. Dufus's feet had a good rest in jail. The Moulton newspaper said that Mr. Dufus McGee, Jr. of Eldorado, Arkansas was captured and later sentenced to five years in the penitentiary for stealing bicycles and other things. Maybe he would go back to Arkansas when he got out of the pen. Harley sure wished he would.

Now that the crooks were all put in jail, the dog returned and the treasure found, what was the next thing Harley needed to do? First, Harley and his daddy had to find where the closest Wells Fargo bank was and make a visit to it. They were told by the Mt. Hope bank president that there was a Wells Fargo bank in Florence, Alabama.

Since Harley was still out of school for A.E.A. and his daddy was still on his vacation, they took off to Florence on Friday morning. They found the bank and went in and asked to see the man in charge. They were led back into a big office and were welcomed in by the president of the bank. Harley told him the whole story about the cave and his dreams about the treasure. When he finished his story about finding the bundles of bills with the Wells Fargo name on the bands around them, he laid the sack of money on the bankers desk.

Needless to say the man's eyes got as big as saucers and he couldn't speak for a little while. Finally he said that he had heard that the bank they were in had been robbed about forty years ago, and that they had never found the money. After looking at the money and making sure that it was real, Mr. Ed, the banker, asked Harley and his daddy if they would come back in about an hour that he had some business t to attend to. They said they would go down to Dusty Joe's cafe and have some dinner and come back by the bank. Mr. Ed thanked them for their honesty and they left the bank.

Harley enjoyed the hamburger, french fries and a big orange drink at Dusty Joe's. His daddy was too nervous to eat. He wondered why the banker wanted them to come back by the bank. He knew that they had been honest about the whole thing. He realized that their story did sound like a fairy tale, but it was all true.

After they had finished eating, they drove back up to the big bank. When they went inside, there were flashbulbs flashing and newspapermen were all over the place. They were asked to come over by a group of dressed up men. They were introduced to the directors and officers of the bank. Mr. Ed wanted Harley and his daddy to pose with them to make a picture.

As the picture was being made, the bank president presented Harley with a reward check for $5,000. The newspapermen asked Harley a lot of questions about finding the money and other things. About all Harley could say was that the money was not his and that the right thing to do was to give it to who it really belonged to. When he was asked what he would do with the reward, he said that he would give $500 of it to his church and probably would save the rest to go to a college that he had been told about by his agriculture teacher.

The next day Harley Earle's and his daddy's picture was on the front page of the Florence paper and the Moulton paper. The headline read, 'Harley Earle sets example for all'.

The story went on to tell about how the Mt. Hope boy had indeed been a model for all to go by.

The days ahead were hard for Harley. He got so much attention from everyone that it was difficult to keep from getting the big head. He even got mail from people that he had never heard of. There were letters from the governor, the local judge, his teachers and even from his Uncle Fred who lived out in Texas. They all said that they were glad to see that he had set the pattern for other young people to follow. Soon, school would be out and he would have a whole summer to fish, ride his new horse, Flicka, and climb mountains. He could hardly wait until next year when he would be in the ninth grade. The main thing he couldn't wait for was the time he would again be in Soapstone Cave.

Printed in the United States
51502LVS00003B/10-168

9 781598 2423